The Antique Clock

A LESLIE LARUE MYSTERY

Molly Owen

I dedicate this book to my late husband, the love of my life. In memory of wonderful times spent in the French Quarter.

ACKNOWLEDGMENTS

Although the French Quarter brings to mind many memories I would not be able to write about this unusual place without the help of the internet and books purchased when staying there. Memories of the decadent buildings and the taste of food only New Orleans can combine in flavors seldom enjoyed is the inspiration for this series. Even though the streets of the French Quarter can convey beauty and excitement, they also bring forth mysteries. It is a culture, unlike any other meshing French, Cajun, Creole, Spanish and Arcadians into a stewpot of colorful history. The challenge in describing this place in the memories of my mind is to surround my readers with the spirit of the searching souls found in the locals, the people that make the French Quarter.

I want to thank those readers who share many wonderful comments on my first Journey with Leslie LaRue in *The Lost Medallion*. Their encouraging words inspire me to continue the series. A special thank you goes to, David for his thoughtfulness (he gave me a special pen for signing my books) and to Steven

Molly Owen

and Amy for their encouragement and enthusiasm that keeps me writing as they anxiously await the second book to be published. My faith grows stronger every day surrounded by the Christian fellowship among friends who continue to have my back through this writing process and remind me to stay on task. Last but not least a big thank you to Janie for another beautiful cover design, editing, and her expertise in getting this copy ready for publication.

Chapter 1

Her hair pulled back in a ponytail, Leslie finished dressing in her usual casual attire, with tan slacks and long white shirt. Looking in the mirror she almost didn't recognize the image of a matron with child. Leslie remembered how young and naïve she was a mire five years ago when she first arrived in New Orleans to finish a novel she was writing. Now married to the love of her life and the mother of an eighteen-month-old, she was more mature, more experienced and hopefully her readers would except the change reflected in her writing.

Sidney, a handsome man with a full head of dark hair beginning to gray at the temples, was as much in love with Leslie today as that day, several years ago, when he saw her for the first time with Annabelle at the bakery. Sidney knew he was attracted to her sweet, casual, scrubbed look, unlike any girl he had known before.

"Are you about ready, hon?" he called to her from their bedroom.

"Almost, give me one more second," she answered changing her mind about tucking in the blouse or wearing on the outside, finally deciding to tuck it in showing off her narrow waist.

"Do we need to get Annabelle on our way?" Sidney asked pulling a plaid shirt from a hanger in the closet.

"No, she said she would take a taxi," Leslie said coming into the bedroom.

"Wow," he said giving her the once over as he buttoned his shirt. "I thought you were just going to have lunch with a girlfriend. Are you sure you're not having an affair with some handsome character?" he said teasing noting the bracelet and neckless set of silver and leather he gave her on her first Mother's Day.

"Oh, sure and I'm having my handsome husband take me to the meeting place. I think I'm a little smarter than that my love," she said giving him a quick peck on the cheek, "we had better hurry, or I'll be late."

"I thought so. We both know Annabelle is always late, so young lady why the hurry if you're not meeting someone else?" he winked at her.

*****

As was her usual habit Annabelle a well-known local attorney, was running late after a long morning of research in preparation for an important meeting later in the day. Annabelle was anxious to see her friend Leslie; however, she was acutely aware her news could not be shared just yet. Checking herself in the hall mirror she adjusted her long black skirt and pulled down the pure white blouse cinched in with a wide white belt matching her hat, gloves and shoes. Grabbing her purse and briefcase she left her home and ran down the alley between her building and the one next door. Locking the gate to the walkway she went out on the sidewalk and began to weave in and out among the many tourist, then hailed a taxi and headed to a little-known place in the Garden District on the edge of the French Quarter in New Orleans where the locals hung out.

Entering Magazine Street, the taxi came to a stop in front of a café and juice bar. After paying her fare she entered the brightly colored, quint building then scanning the room full of the lunch crowd sitting in bent wood chairs at round tables, she spotted Leslie sitting towards the back next to the kitchen. Leslie waved then stood up to greet Annabelle with a big smile.

"Hi Leslie," Annabelle said giving her a tight hug. "I'm so glad to see you."

"You too. I've really missed you Annabelle," Leslie said.

"Yes, it's been way too long, and we must stop doing that, I know we're both busy but surly we can make time for each other."

"You're right, from now on we'll just have to do a better job," Leslie said.

"Leslie, how's my God son doing?" she said removing her hat and gloves then sitting down in the chair across the table.

"Oh Annabelle, he's into everything, walking, talking. Sidney and I adore him. Ryan is such a little man. So much like his father. Full of energy and surprises. But enough about my favorite subject. How are you? Busy?"

"Yeah, and you won't believe what's going to happen today. It's right up your alley, Leslie. Full of intrigue with all the bells and whistles, this one has the makings of a good book," she said a little weary.

"Well, I need to finish writing this book first, not easy with super baby around. Daisy, our nanny, tries to corral him but I'm still distracted even behind closed doors. We're thinking about building a studio out back just for me to have a place to write."

"Your old cottage is empty; you could set up office there." Annabelle said handing the menu back to the waiter.

"I wish," Leslie said remembering her time in the cottage behind Annabelle's home in the French Quarter.

"No, Leslie I'm serious, why not? I know you'd be away from Ryan, but you could get a lot more work done in half the time. Think about it."

"What's happening today that you think would make a good book?" she said changing the subject.

"I can't reveal anything right now. I have an appointment with the family this afternoon and I must tell you I'm not looking forward to this meeting. I have to give them some news they aren't expecting," Annabelle said.

"What kind of news?" Leslie said curious.

"Let's just say they're not going to be happy. I just hope they don't shoot the messenger," Annabelle said laughing.

"Well, I certainly hope not. Is it that bad?"

"Afraid so," Annabelle said removing her white gloves in anticipation of their food arriving.

Two orders of Jambalaya filled with Cajun spices came and in between bites, they caught up on each other's lives. Noting the time, Annabelle put her spoon down then getting up from the table she gathered her things. Giving Leslie one last hug she said, "I've got the bill. I'd better get a move on. It's been fun… like old times. Think about what I said about the cottage."

"Okay, I'll talk to Sidney and let you know. Thanks for lunch and have a great day, this has been wonderful. Let's do it again soon. And, Annabelle, you're in my prayers for a good outcome at this mysterious meeting you're having," Leslie said grinning as they left the cashier and walked out onto the sidewalk where Annabelle hailed a taxi while Leslie walked to the car where Sidney had arrived to give her a ride back home.

She leaned over as Sidney gave her a kiss on the cheek.

"So, how's Annabelle? Did you gals catch up on all the gossip?" Sidney asked pulling out into the street.

"She's great, the same Annabelle, hat gloves and big brimmed hat, and she had something to tell me about a client but couldn't tell me until after their meeting this afternoon. She said it had all the makings of a good book."

"Well, that's intriguing. I wonder if she'll get me involved." Sidney said.

Sidney's Detective Agency was doing well. So, he hired another agent, Charles Bodet, which he had worked with in the FBI, to help with the growing business. They did investigative work for Annabelle on occasion. Although she was an excellent investigator in her own right, she knew she could trust Sidney especially for the more serious investigations involving major crimes. They had a good working relationship, and Sidney was glad for the business.

*****

Before the arrival of the Bordeaux family, Annabelle put God in charge, knowing that whatever went on at the meeting, it would be in His hands not hers. *Father, I praise You and thank You for Your glory that surrounds me in everything I do. Be with me as I give this news to the Bordeaux family and Lord be with each of them, give them strength as they absorb what I'm about to tell them. I pray this in Jesus' name. Amen.* It was a typical Bordeaux family gathering, totally disconnected, with Katrina Louise late as usual and Sandy asking a million questions as one by one, family members entered Annabelle's law office.

Sandy and husband Robert Bordeaux had moved far away from New Orleans, as far as they could to get away from the Bordeaux clan and were not happy about the call to the lawyer's office. Sandy with sun-damaged skin and blazing red hair was demanding answers to this imposition and she wanted those answers now. While tall, handsome, though a little on the heavy side, husband Robert Bordeaux third in line of siblings, could care less what Sandy had to say he just wanted her to shut up. Their relationship as husband and wife, or on any level for that matter, was rocky at best, making it difficult for others to be around them.

Rose Marie, second to the oldest, a God-fearing woman whose appearance had stayed pretty much the same in a short-bobbed graying hairdo framing her ageless face. With her husband Patrick Murphy, Irish to the core, average height, a mature look of authority, they had raised their family of three children in an upscale neighborhood on the outskirts of the French Quarter in the same home they purchased in their early marriage. Catholic born and bred, Rose Marie and Patrick had found their faith challenged. While seeking another path for their beliefs, they joined a Bible-based fellowship, a small group of Christians that studied scripture.

Jonathon Bordeaux, tall and lanky with salt and pepper hair reseeding at the temple was the oldest of the bunch and closest to Rose Marie born only months apart, had arrived about the same time Sandy and Robert. But he held back long enough for them to go ahead of him so as not to expose himself to a barrage of questions he was sure Sandy would throw his way. He had not seen much of the family as of late and was not anxious to spend any amount of time with them now.

A.J., (Ann Judith Bordeaux Smith Greenland) the baby of the family, was divorced for the second time and begrudgingly left with being the single mom of three children, two by Smith and one by Greenland that cramped her lifestyle of wild parties. Sitting in Annabelle's office, she was shamelessly dressed like a common streetwalker with a cleavage-revealing neckline that would surely expose mounds of flesh with one deliberate lean toward her lap. Her hemline crept up to just below the point of no return showing her long bare legs crossed with a high heel clad foot swinging impatiently in the air.

Jeffrey Bordeaux and Katrina Louise Bordeaux, born fourth and fifth in sibling order and only two years apart in age, both single, dedicated, career-oriented business people were seemingly very content in their individual lives. Jeffrey, tall with a ruddy complexion, a hint of graying throughout his head of black hair and one of New Orleans's most eligible bachelors, sat back in the corner with thumbs flying over the little screen, texting split-second decisions for his very successful business as he rudely separated himself from the conversation in the room.

Suddenly with a grand entrance, the strikingly beautiful Katrina Louise arrived, dressed in her best "going-to-sell-a-house outfit" even though a bit frazzled, and apologetic for her tardiness as she took a seat by Jeffrey who gave her a quick hug and halfway smirking smile.

Watching Katrina Louise take her seat next to Jeffrey, Annabelle, sat behind her large mahogany desk with her hands folded in front of her, exposing her manicured fingernails polished in bright red that complemented the stark white blouse, accentuating her cameo face with bright red lipstick, deep blue eyes and black hair pulled back in a chignon. Her Hollywood beauty not wasted for one minute on Robert as he couldn't take his eyes off her. She surveyed the room and noted the group before her as she waited for everyone's attention before proceeding to announce she had important information to share with them.

"Now that everyone is here, I can begin with the reason I summoned you for this meeting," she said.

"Well, it's about time. I'd like to know what's so confounded important that we all have to be here. We already had a reading of the will. Is the estate finally settled? We haven't heard a word since the old folks died." Sandy spouted in her usual outspoken Southern drawl manner.

"Sandy!" Robert growled puffy face turning red.

"What? "Sandy said glaring at her spouse.

"Just for once keep your mouth shut," he said.

Sandy turned with a flip of her red hair and started to retaliate when Annabelle cleared her throat in an attempt to interrupt whatever was going on between Sandy and Robert.

Now with all eyes focused on her, Annabelle said, "the bank that holds the second mortgage on the house in the Bordeaux Family Trust called me because my late father was the attorney on record. She told me the second mortgage came due and, on further scrutiny, the bank has determined the trust's assets are missing, and an investigation is in progress to ascertain the whereabouts of these assets."

"A second mortgage? Why did the folks take out a second mortgage?" Rose Marie asked.

"It was a line of credit using the house for collateral," Annabelle replied.

"What do you mean 'missing'? Everything? Stocks, bonds, everything? How can that be?" Rose Marie said turning to Jonathon, "Did you know about this?"

Before he could answer, Robert shouted, "He better well know about it. That's all I've got to say. Haven't you been watching this? Did you let this just dribble away? Weren't you watching the stock market? What's the matter with you man?"

Suddenly the room filled with accusations as first one then another tried to make sense of what they heard.

"It'll be alright, aren't there protections, you know government guarantees to the banks, stuff like that?" Sandy said hopefully, looking at Annabelle for answers.

"You're so stupid, your brain isn't big enough to figure this one out, babe. So, just sit there and put a sock in it," Robert shouted at her.

Jeffrey spoke up, "Robert, that's enough, there's nothing we can do until the investigation is complete, and for all we know there could've been a hacker into the trust account. We can speculate all we want but until they finish the audit and I'm assuming the FBI will be called in, there's not much we can do. Isn't that right, Annabelle?"

"Jeffrey's right. All you can do now is wait for the investigation to be completed and pray they find answers soon." Annabelle said.

"Pray? Really like that'll do any good," Sandy said under her breath.

"Did Jonathon leave? When did he leave, I wanted to talk to him, I know he must be devastated since he was supposed to be taking care of the trust." Rose Marie said trying to keep her brain working as she thought about the many ramifications the news brought to herself and her siblings.

*****

Jonathon hurried to his car hoping no one saw him sneak out of Annabelle's office. He couldn't breathe, and his heart was pounding against his ribs screaming to get out like a caged animal. Brain freeze was the pain he felt, like with a sudden swallow of cold ice cream, with his thoughts whirling around in his skull. *'Stop, think, relax, take it easy'* he told himself as he reached for the door handle of the car only to find it locked, *'of course, you idiot, you don't leave your car unlocked on the street,'* he chastised himself, then fumbling for his keys he promptly dropped them on the ground. His hands were sweaty, and his fingers were numbing as again, then again, he tried to retrieve his keys, finally the door unlocked, he climbed in and turned the key, putting the gearshift in reverse he maneuvered the car back and forth out of the parking space nearly creaming a van parked behind him. Shifting into drive he stepped on the gas pedal and headed straight to his condominium.

The streets were crowded creating first one delay and then another as he maneuvered through the traffic. It got even worse as he approached the colorful European style French Quarter alive with fresh aromas from many restaurants surrounding tourist while they made their choices between sweet, savory and spicy creole. Musicians occupied every corner, swaying to the soulful sounds coming from trumpets, trombones, harmonicas and banjos as they competed for air space. Visitors stopped to listen then tossed money into the tins while locals scurried among them to their destinations. Horns honked while pedestrians and cars competed for the streets. The celebration atmosphere annoyed him, for he knew he had nothing to celebrate.

Finally, able to park, he ran to the gate that led to the courtyard. He hurried across the open space around a fountain and up the spiral staircase to the place he had called home for the last few months. Still shaking, his fingers managed to turn the key in the door. He ran, two steps at a time, upstairs. Grabbing clothes from their hangers, he threw them in the suitcases he had laid out on the bed. He put the safe deposit box key in the pocket of one of the shirts and headed downstairs. The sound of the buzzer at the gate sent his blood pressure up and his heart racing.

Setting the suitcases down, he answered the intercom to his condominium then heard the words he had dreaded. He never truly believed it would happen but now he was forced to face it.

"Mr. Bordeaux, it's the police, open up."

He threw the suitcases into the hall closet and went back outside, down the spiral stairs across the courtyard and to the gate.

"What's this about?" he asked.

"Sir you need to come with us. The DA has some questions for you."

Chapter 2

Several days after Leslie's conversation with Annabelle, she and Sidney discussed the pros and cons of leaving Ryan with the nanny while Leslie worked on her book in the French Quarter. After praying about it, they decided to give it a try, so Leslie packed up her laptop and headed for the little cottage she once called home.

She missed the French Quarter where she became friends with Annabelle and fell in love with Sidney. A novel she was working on at the time led her to this private place to write without interruptions. She missed walking to the drugstore owned by her friends, Joe and Sadie Sully, who had introduced her to a group of believers that held church meetings in individual homes. Now, she and Sidney had started their own group of believers that met in their home.

This romantic place was where she and Sidney had started their lives together as husband and wife. Before Ryan was born, they moved from the cute little cottage behind Annabelle's home, after Leslie finished two novels, to the Garden District where they started renovation on one of the old Victorian houses on St. Charles Avenue. Leslie continued to write in spite of the many distractions.

The ride down St. Charles Avenue gave Leslie time to regroup from mommy to writer as she mentally put her thoughts together mesmerized by the click clack of the streetcar melting with the sounds of a fog horn in the distance and the church bells from the St. Louis Cathedral. Watching the scenery of large homes surrounded by lush gardens encased behind wrought iron fences, ideas began to churn in anticipation and making a few notes on her notepad, she anxiously waited to put them on her laptop.

Her first day back brought many memories as she turned Annabelle's extra key in the lock of the iron-gate, smiling as she remembered her first frightening encounter with Sidney. At the time, she was unaware that God had a hand in their meeting and Sidney would be the man she prayed for and eventually married. It was like old times being back in the French Quarter in the quaint little cottage separated by the colorful courtyard full of tropical plants and trees behind Annabelle's house where she found peace and inspiration to write. She grabbed a fruit from the lemon tree before letting herself into this space of respite to continue writing the book she hoped would be finished in a short amount of time.

*****

Both busy with work, it had been days since the two friends had time to catch up. Annabelle's law practice was keeping her occupied and Leslie was hard at work on the manuscript of her latest book. However, today she was meeting Annabelle at la Madeleine, just like times passed, for beignets and a hot thick cup of java laced with chicory.

"Good Morning, Ms. Robicheaux."

"Good Morning, Mrs. Rye," Annabelle answered giving Leslie a tight hug as they shared a laugh remembering their first meeting in the very same place, at the very same table.

"We had no idea that hot sticky morning where our relationship would lead us," Leslie said sitting down across the table from Annabelle.

"We most certainly didn't," Annabelle said taking off her white gloves and laying them on the table.

"Oh, Annabelle, you're such the Southern bell," Leslie remarked shaking her head. "But don't you ever change, you hear, I just won't have it. I love you the way you are, white gloves, wide rim hat and all."

"Why, thank you, Leslie," a little embarrassed. "But enough about me, how is it going with the book?"

"Very well, actually. You were right. I can get a lot more done. Once I got used to being away from Ryan that is. Daisy is so good with him, she takes him to the park, which he loves, and we are very fortunate to have her as our nanny," she said taking a sip of coffee. "So, tell me more about this mystery of yours."

Annabelle sat up folded her hands on the table in front of her then leaned closer to her friend and began to tell her the story without divulging the identity of the family because she knew how it could affect Leslie.

"This family had engaged my father many years before, to oversee the legal aspects of their trust. The parents had complete control of the trust as long as they were living, however their oldest son also had power of attorney and his signature on their accounts," Annabelle began.

"Before their deaths, it appears as if the son managed to take out a home equity loan against his parents' house. I discovered that his business was in trouble," she said careful not to reveal the nature of his business. "So, he may have convinced them it was the only way they could help him save his business." Annabelle told Leslie.

"Now it's time to settle the estate and the money is gone and the house is in foreclosure. The authorities suspected the son from the beginning but needed proof. These are facts yet to be disclosed to the family. At the meeting with them, I had to play it cool hoping the son didn't suspect they were onto him."

"This is going to take a while, isn't it? And how are you going to be paid, if there's no money?" Leslie said across the table with concern about her friend.

"That's a good question," Annabelle said shrugging her shoulders. "I'm not sure what role I'll play in all of this. The family hasn't hired me. This is the first dealings I've had with them. My Dad was the one that set up the trust. I took over a lot of his clients after his death. But when I lost most of them several years ago, I had to dissolve his practice. I rebuilt my clientele and opened my own practice. So, we'll see where this goes?"

"I guess we never know what some people are really capable of doing."

"How true and now I've called the family for another meeting to give them more news they don't want to hear about their brother's arrest and upcoming arraignment in which he's accused of embezzlement," Annabelle said gathering her purse and gloves.

The two women left the bakery and walked together across the street to the gate that opened to the walkway between the two buildings. Reaching the courtyard, they gave each other a hug then parted, each going her own way.

Leslie poured a cup of tea, went to the desk, pulled out her laptop and began to type. Soon she was in the groove as her thoughts carried her far away from the reality of the day and into the world of intrigue and adventure. This would be her fifth published novel and the excitement built as each new chapter ended.

Looking up from her work she waved as Annabelle left for what Leslie assumed was her meeting with the family. *What a mess* she thought as her fingers stopped typing and her creative mind wondered from the book to the situation Annabelle found herself. The ringing of her cell phone brought her back to the present.

"Hello Hubby, what's up?"

"Just checking on you."

"Really, are you across the street or on the roof looking at me?"

"Neither, I'm at the gate."

"Oh, I see that old gate trick again, well, Mr. Rye, I'm not sure I know you well enough to unlock the gate. Have we been properly introduced?"

They both laughed as Leslie walked toward the gate remembering the first time they met when she forgot to lock the gate and Sidney walked in behind her to introduce himself and scared her half to death. That started a very rocky journey to where they were today.

"Hello, Mrs. Rye," Sidney said giving Leslie a quick peck on the cheek as he went through the gate.

"Hello yourself," she said securing the gate behind them.

"How about some lunch?" he said walking with her down the walkway to the open courtyard.

"That sounds great, let me save my work and I'll be ready," Leslie said running ahead.

"I just saw Annabelle leave, where's she off to in such a hurry?" He said leaning down to smell the blossom of an oleander.

"Probably going to her office uptown, you won't believe what she told me this morning."

"Really, gossip or a case?

"A case, I'll tell you all about it over lunch, I'm hungry for a po'boy, how about you?"

"Let's do it."

They hailed a taxi and headed for Johnny's Po-Boy on St Louis Street for, according to Sidney, some of the best po'boy in New Orleans.

Sitting next to each other at a table for two on the sidewalk, they watched the excitement surrounding them with street mimes, jugglers and people selling Mardi Gras beads. Soon their sandwiches came, and between bites, Leslie shared the information learned from Annabelle earlier.

"Boy, how can anyone look in the mirror after doing something like that to one's own family?" Sidney said shaking his head.

"I know," Leslie said wiping the food residue from her lips with a napkin.

"It would be rather hard to get your head around something as awful as the betrayal of your own flesh and blood. You can't help but wonder what makes people do what they do. You know I see a lot of that sort of thing in my business. And, you know Les, that's what keeps me in business is people like that, doing illegal or immoral things, thinking they can get away with it. They must realize they will be caught eventually."

"I know, and look at the pain these people leave behind, broken promises, broken lives… everything. My prayer is the family turns to God for strength and guidance as they deal with this. And, it may take a while to sort out. Especially with their sibling facing embezzling charges and jail time," Leslie said as she and Sidney walked down Decatur Street toward Jackson Square. Passing a shade spot Leslie turned to Sidney then taking his hand she led him to the bench under the tree.

"We really need to pray for this family Sid, my intuition tells me there's more to this story than Annabelle divulged."

They bowed their heads and each in their own words asked God to bring strength, understanding and peace to the situation this family found themselves in, and to put forgiveness in their hearts. Sidney closed the prayer with a quote from the bible, *"In John 16:33 Jesus said, 'You'll have trouble. But take heart. I have overcome the world.' Lord we ask the Holy Spirit to put that verse on the hearts of these hurting people. We ask in His Holy name. Amen."*

They continued to walk holding hands bathed in the assurance that God was in control. Sidney hailed a taxi. On their arrival, holding the door for her he asked the driver to wait for him and took her to the gate. "One thing is for certain. Annabelle will do a good job representing the family–pay or no pay. That's just who she is," he told Leslie.

"She isn't sure about that, yet. Even though the family trust was initiated by Annabelle's father, she really doesn't represent them. The only reason she's involved is her bank was also her father's and he was the lawyer of record," Leslie told Sidney as she shut the gate.

"Well, I sure wouldn't want to be in Annabelle's shoes right now."

"Me neither," Leslie said through the gate.

"I love you Les. See you tonight."

Chapter 3

The second meeting with the Bordeaux family was not much different from the first meeting. The more time they had to reflect on the situation, the more confused and angry they became. They had just learned that their parent's beautiful Garden District home was now in foreclosure due to non-payment of the equity loan, and that all the bank accounts were empty including the safe deposit box where their mother's jewelry had been. Their bleak future loomed in front of them like a huge monster ready to devoir them.

"Now that everyone is here, we can begin with the reason I called all of you for this meeting," Annabelle said.

"Wait, Jonathon isn't here," Rose Marie said of her older brother. "I haven't been able to reach him for days."

"Jonathon won't be here, that's what I need to tell you," Annabelle said with obvious concern in her voice.

"Is he alright? Has something happened to him?" Rose Marie asked first looking at Patrick then at the others.

Annabelle paused then as gently as she knew how told the family gathered in front of her that Jonathon was part of the investigation and a warrant was served accusing him of embezzling all of the family's inheritance and that he was now in custody at the Orleans Parish City Jail awaiting arraignment.

The pin-dropping silence in the room deafened the occupants until a few gasps by Sandy who after catching her breath, gargled out a few choice words of utter hatred until Robert turned on her and told her clearly, to shut up.

Rose Marie, in disbelief that the person she knew as her older brother and best friend growing up, could possibly commit such a crime argued that it was impossible. "Jonathon? He would do no such thing. He was the executor of the estate," she paused to think things through as she realized why he had not been answering her calls, "but if he has done this" she continued, "he had a good reason, and besides aren't there some laws or something that would keep him from taking all of our money?"

"I'm afraid the law doesn't keep this from happening because he had the power of attorney. The law only protects you before the fact, a red flag earlier could have prevented this. However, Jonathon was clever, and the bank didn't discover the discrepancy until recently," Annabelle told them.

"What kind of red flag?" Rose Marie asked.

Annabelle tried to answer but the loud accusations drowned her out, and the commotion in front of her took her attention as she listened to the reaction of each sibling.

A. J., for the first time, seemed to crumble into a pile of hidden reality putting her legs down and moving her chair back from the rest of the group. All her efforts at sexuality with her long hair draping around her bare shoulders and her flesh revealing dress seemed to go unnoticed. Her face went ashen as she attempted to speak. The words stuck in her throat not allowing them to leave her mouth, she muttered a syllable, then another, until she stopped trying, and shaking her head, she put her hands in her lap staring at them like a little girl.

Jeffrey looked at Katrina Louise then at his siblings and said, "Why are we all so surprised?"

Katrina Louise nodded her head in agreement. "He has been very absorbed in himself lately, this is what happens when you hide from the obvious and honestly we should've seen it coming. It's been almost two years and not a one of us has seen a dime. Our parents gave him the control as the oldest and we just sat back and let him run with it, so as I see it, it's our own fault."

"Well, I never thought he would stoop so low as to steal from his own brothers and sisters, the lousy son of a b ..." Robert said with anger bringing red to his face. "Who does he think he is anyway? Wait until I get my hands on him. I'll get our money back if I have to beat it out of him."

"Robert, please don't talk like that, mom and dad wouldn't want us to turn on our own flesh and blood like that," Rose Marie said hoping to defuse her brother's innate temper.

"Good grief, Rose Marie, did you hear what Annabelle said, Jonathon is the one that turned on his own flesh and blood, and he deserves every ounce of hatred we can give him. I get so sick of your goody, goody attitude. Put all that sweetie, religious stuff in a closet somewhere and come out here into the real world," Robert shouted at her.

"Now just a minute, Robert, that's enough. Don't take it out on your sister. It's not her fault. We just don't want this to get out of hand. Name-calling is not going to help the situation. Let's just all calm ourselves and see if there is anything we can do about this at this point." Patrick said noticing the tears welling up in Rose Marie's eyes in disbelief.

Just then, A. J. got up and ran out of the room with her hands over her mouth. Katrina Louise followed her to the restroom. After A. J. regurgitated in the toilet, Katrina Louise wet a paper towel and wiped A. J.'s face.

"Are you okay?" she asked.

"No, I was really counting on that money sis, I had big plans, you know buy a new car, maybe take a fancy trip and now it is all ruined."

"I know A. J., I'm sorry."

"How could he do this? Why did he do this to me?"

"I wish I could give you an answer that made sense, A. J., but I don't have the answer for sure."

"You think he was just greedy."

"Yes, but I don't really know what he was using the money for, was he just spending it, you know what I mean?"

"No"

"Well, was he broke, did he have debt from his business or maybe medical bills, was he sick and needed the money for an operation? Why did he need to steal that money?" she asked leaving the restroom with A.J.

A.J. looked at her with a blank stare not wanting to think about any problems Jonathon may have, she was too busy wallowing in her own self-pity.

Back in Annabelle's office things had calmed down somewhat and she told them Jonathon's arraignment was the next Monday to face the embezzlement charges. She again told them if the charges held up he could go to jail.

"What about mother's antiques, her precious china and silver, her collection of paintings?" Rose Marie questioned.

"Indications are that most of it is gone and what's left will be sold to settle the estate. There are still unpaid bills that will have to be paid."

"Bills for what?" Sandy yelled

"According to the findings of the investigation, Jonathon purchased several things, and took trips he charged on your parent's credit cards," Annabelle told them.

"Oh, it just doesn't end, does it? Not one of us suspected anything. That's what we get for being so trusting." Katrina Louise said.

"It's ended for me. I don't know what I'm going to do. How will I live without that money? I waited my whole life for that inheritance, if I had known this was going to happen, well, I wouldn't have gotten a divorce. Now I guess I'll have to get a job and support my kids," A. J. said.

"Well, now that's a concept, you beat all A. J., you with your little pity party. You could always get a job and let your ex's have the kids and the alimony and child support. Believe me those kids of yours would do a lot better with those guys and their girlfriends for a mother than the likes of you," Robert said spitting out each word of venom as he spoke to his younger sister pushing away Rose Marie's hand on his arm. "You probably received more of mom and dad's money when they were alive bailing you out of first one thing and then another, than we would've ever received from the estate, so missy you can just go on being the slut you are."

"Robert that's enough," Rose Marie said firmly, standing up between her two siblings. "We're all in a very vulnerable state right now and the worst thing we can do is turn on each other, we need to pray," she said bowing her head.

Robert, not in the mood for any God thing, headed for the door ahead of everyone with Sandy close behind. A.J. with head down low left still in shock. Katrina Louise gave Jeffrey a hug then left making sure A.J. was okay. Rose Marie began to pray aloud. *Our almighty loving Father, we lay this before You knowing You'll give us peace and understanding. Be with Jonathon, Lord. And Jesus, help this family not turn on each other but look to you for guidance. In Jesus' name, we pray. Amen.* Annabella and Patrick joined in with Amen and thanked Rose Marie for her prayer as she and Patrick followed her family out the door.

Everyone was gone except for Jeffrey, the youngest son who was still sitting in the chair at the back of the room. Sitting up, he cleared his throat then said, "What'll happen to Jonathon if he's found guilty?"

Annabelle, struck by his apparent concern while also noticing like his older brothers he was quite handsome, explained the process and ended with the worst scenario being a ten- to fifteen-year jail sentence probably in a minimum-security facility for white-collar prisoners.

Leaning forward with his elbows on his knees he put his forehead in his hands, then slowing raising his head he began to share his thoughts.

"What do you think caused him to do this? Debt from Doris's cancer, illness he didn't share with us? What makes a person do something like this? I agree with Rose Marie, this is not the

Jonathon I know. I just can't imagine what possessed him to do this. Surely he knew he was committing a criminal act."

Annabelle could see the hurt, concern and frustration and wanted to say something, anything to help him but she didn't have an explanation and was not about to speculate.

"I'm truly sorry for what has happened to your family and your brother Jonathon, and I wish I could say something to ease your pain, but I don't have any answers. At this point, Jonathon is the only one with answers to those questions. We'll just have to wait and see what develops," she said as compassionately as she could.

When Jeffrey left Annabelle looked up, then bowing her head she began to pray. *Gracious Heavenly Father be with this family, give them peace. There is so much disconnect with each of them as they have grown apart from each other and from You Lord. I pray You'll keep them in your sight as they face the coming days. Lord Jesus, led me in the path of righteousness that I may be a light to them. I pray In Jesus' name. Amen.*

Chapter **4**

A devoted Christian, Patrick relied on the Holy Spirit to show him the way in times of need. Aware of God's promise, he remembered Paul's letter to Philemon and knew God was his partner and would walk with him, Jonathon, and the family though this crisis. *Perhaps this will help Jonathon to rebuild a relationship with You, Lord. After all, we never know what Your plan is*, he thought.

He sat at his desk in his home office looking out the window at the side yard, where he had tackled the overgrown flowerbeds, working hard until he had replanted the flowers into a beautiful, lush garden. He and Rose Marie loved this stately two-story house on St. Charles Avenue, not far from where Sidney and Leslie lived. It was not a mansion like the more famous places further away, but it was here they raised their children, and now he was contemplating a move that might put their home of thirty years in jeopardy. But knowing how close his wife had been with Jonathon, growing up, he would do the best he could to make life easier for both of them.

Having already tried reasoning with Robert, he thought the only other sibling with assets would be Jeffrey. Patrick dialed the number to his office. The secretary told him Jeffrey would be out the rest of the day, but she would contact him and make sure he called Patrick as soon as possible. Hanging up the receiver he bowed his head in prayer. *Father, be with Jonathon. Give him strength as he waits for bail and Father give me wisdom to do what's best for Jonathon, and for me and Rose Marie. Thank you, Father. In Jesus' name. Amen.* Startled by the ringing of the phone, he reached for the receiver.

"Hello," Patrick said

"Hi Patrick, what's happening, any news?" Jeffrey said.

"No. Jeffrey, thank you for returning my call so quick. I know you must be real busy. I need help raising money for Jonathon's bail. I have already talked to Robert with no avail. He wants nothing to do with helping Jonathon. The bail is set at one million dollars. Here in Louisiana we have to come up with 12%."

The silence was deafening, as Patrick waited for an answer.

"That's $120,000.00. Does it have to be cash?"

"No, the bondsman said he would take collateral," Patrick replied hopefully.

"I don't know, Patrick, let me think about it, I would have to liquidate some assets. Just let me think about it and I'll get back with you."

"Thanks Jeffrey I appreciate it. Rose Marie and I have equity in our house we can put up, so let me know," Patrick told him.

"I don't like the sound of that Patrick, your home?"

"I wouldn't want to touch the business, it's our lively hood. We can always get another house," Patrick said hoping Jeffrey didn't hear the concern in his voice. "No matter what he's done, we can't leave him in there right now, it's just not humane. Even if he's guilty he will serve in a white-collar prison not a situation for hardened criminals, and the county jail is no picnic either."

"Have you seen him?" Jeffrey asked.

"Yes, have you?"

"No, I just can't bring myself to seeing him behind bars so to speak, I'm sure I wouldn't see him in a cell, but you know, just the thought. I'm going to wait until he returns home, in his condo."

For some reason Patrick got the feeling that Jeffrey was not sure where he stood with the whole situation. After some more conversation about the bail, the two men agreed to talk later.

*****

Today, as unsettled as she felt, she would go to the Orleans Parish City Jail to see Jonathon, who was anxiously waiting for Patrick to arrange bond for his release and for her to give him her support. Soon to celebrate her fiftieth birthday, she was still surprised at how she seemed to have aged overnight as she stood staring at her drawn-face reflection in the bathroom mirror. Tears of disbelief flowed down her makeup-free cheeks landing in the sink below as slowly she bowed her head in prayer asking God to be with her older brother Jonathon. *God, only You know Jonathon's heart. Be with him, give him courage in the face of what's to come. And God be with me, help me say the right thing and show my unconditional love and support for my brother. I love you, Lord. In Jesus' name. Amen*

Born a mere eighteen months apart, she and Jonathon were very close as children. In school she was one year behind him. Rose Marie looked up to her brother and knew he would be there for her always. Now she would be there for him even in the face of the accusation that he embezzled money from the family trust. It wasn't the money or even the lost heritage that bothered her. It was the broken trust.

Patrick was not at all happy about her decision to visit Jonathon in prison, knowing how it would affect her, but he understood her need to support her sibling in spite of the accusations against him. After a brief conversation with Robert, and a subsequent conversation with Jeffrey, it became clear that arranging bail was up to Patrick. His visit with Jonathon the day before was uneventful except for the realization that the bail money wouldn't come from Jonathon since everything he owned was hocked to the max. Pushing questions to the back of his mind, he assured his brother-in-law he would raise the money for his bail.

*****

Sitting in the car outside the City Jail she put her head down on her arms resting on the steering wheel; tears washed her face as sobs took over her being. Her mind filled with the same questions again as she tried to make sense of the facts, as she knew them. Jonathon had not shed any light on the subject as she asked him several times, "why?" Soon the visit came to a close and she threw him a kiss through the glass window and said good-bye hoping he didn't see the disappointment on her face.

Once she regained her composure, she left the parking lot and drove straight to Leslie's house. A look at her swollen face in the rear-view mirror told the whole story but she didn't care as she opened the car door and stood on the sidewalk. Getting her equilibrium, she walked up the steps to the huge glass inlayed door and rang the bell.

"Rose Marie, come in. Are you alright?"

"No, I need your help Leslie, I'm so concerned about my family. Something terrible has happened. This has been an awful blow and I do not see how we will survive."

"Come in here and let's talk. It will help to air your feelings, even though I'm sure all I can do is be your friend Rose Marie and pray with you." Leslie said.

"Thank you, Leslie," she told her the story in bits and pieces. "Patrick is out trying to raise enough money for Jonathon's bail and I just came from seeing Jonathon. Oh, it was awful. I have never seen the inside of a jail before, except on TV. I can't tell you how horrible it was," she said wiping her eyes. "I know I look frightful, I can't seem to quit crying."

"Let me get us something to drink, the powder room is right around the corner if you want to wash your face. It might help," Leslie said with her arms around Rose Marie's shoulders helping her up from the chair and leading her to the door of the small bathroom under the stairs near the kitchen.

Still mulling Rose Marie's story over in her mind, she put two and two together. The family Annabelle told her about was the family of their close friends, the Murphy's, Patrick and Rose Marie. Leslie placed the silver tray with hot tea and teacups on the table in front of the divan and pouring the hot tea into a cup set it in front of Rose Marie who seemed to be doing a little better as she took deep breaths to stop the sobs.

"Do you have any idea if your brother Jonathon was in some kind of trouble and maybe that's the reason behind all of this?"

"Actually, from all indications, what with the cars, boats, condo, vacations and all the other things that ran up the bills, it appears to be greed." Rose Marie said with disgust in her voice. "And that's what's so puzzling, Jonathon has never been flamboyant or even a partier. He has always been quiet, reserved and satisfied with what he had like Able, you know Adam's good son in the Bible, whereas Robert was more like Cain. I would almost expect that from Robert but not Jonathon. After Doris died, he became a recluse, stayed to himself. He and Doris never traveled much, they were real homebodies and seemed to like it that way. They never had children, and Doris never worked. They lived a modest life. His little clock repair business seemed to sustain them. We didn't see much of Jonathon after Mom and Dad died." Rose Marie said looking off into space. "Maybe if we had been more involved in his life the past few years we would know more about what caused this."

"Is Jonathon a believer?"

"We all went to church growing up but he and Doris didn't go to church after they got married. That always worried mom especially when Doris got sick with cancer. When Doris died, Jonathon decided to hold the service at the funeral home. So, I guess the answer to your question is…I don't know."

"Did Doris have an insurance policy?"

"I don't know. I know so little about Jonathon. I just didn't realize how much we had grown apart and why didn't I try harder to bring Jonathon back to Christ. I'm so sorry I neglected to help him."

Rose Marie, don't blame yourself, don't dwell on regrets try to find the good in all of this. God will be there for you. Matthew 11: 28 says *come to me all you who labor and are heavy laden, and I'll give you rest.* Own that verse Rose Marie, and it'll see you through. It's not too late to help Jonathon, to bring him back to Christ. Would you like to pray with me?" Leslie said holding each of Rose Marie's hands as she prayed. *Father we praise You, we glorify Your holy name. Thank you, God, for the blessing of our faithful friend. We come to You with heavy hearts. We know You're in control of this situation. We ask for strength and courage in the coming days for Jonathon and his family. Give Rose Marie peace as she faces the events that are unfolding. We love you, God. In Jesus' precious name. Amen."*

"Thank you, Leslie, you've been a great blessing. Thank you so much," she said giving Leslie a tight hug before leaving.

Leslie watched as Rose Marie went to her car then went back to the kitchen to find Ryan sitting in his high chair ready for dinner. She reached over, took his small pudgy cheeks in her hands, and kissed the top of his head as he squealed and reached for her to pick him up. Lifting him out of his high chair, she twirled him around and hugged him with the smell of baby powder filling her nostrils.

"Did you have a good nap Ryan? Thank you, Daisy, for giving Miss Rose Marie and me some privacy."

"No problem Miss Leslie. I hope Miss Rose Marie is alright."

"She will be just fine won't she, Ryan? God will take good care of her."

"He has been a very good boy today, we went to the park, read stories, and took a bath. He's such a joy to care for Miss Leslie." Daisy said watching Leslie enjoy her little boy. "Mr. Sidney called and said he may be a little late, something about a case he's working on."

"Thank you, Daisy, you can go now if you'd like and I'll see you first thing in the morning. Give Daisy a kiss Ryan, tell her bye-bye," Leslie encouraged. "Thank you again, Daisy."

After walking Daisy to the front of the house to wave goodbye, Leslie shut and locked the large heavy door weighted down by the beveled glass insert. The setting sun began to cast shades of pink across the sky, peeking through the trees lining St. Charles Avenue in front of their home. The glass sparkled with the glistening light from the sun surrounding her with warmth as she again lifted Rose Marie and her family up to God.

She took Ryan back to the kitchen where she put him on her lap and began to feed him. Her mind wondered to her conversation with Rose Marie. Thinking back about some things Annabelle had told her earlier, she wondered how the meeting had gone with the other members of the Bordeaux family.

Fall was in the air and darkness filled the house with shadows as she tucked Ryan away in his crib. Leslie bathed and wrapping her hair in a towel, she settled in for some work on the book. Sometime later she looked up over her glasses to see Sidney standing in the doorway.

"Hi, how long have you been standing there?"

"Long enough," Sidney said teasing.

"Long enough for what?"

"To thank God that you're my wife and the mother of our son."

"Oh," she said taking her glasses off and laying them on the nightstand next to the bed. "We really are so blessed, Sid. I thank God every day for the two men in my life."

"Who is the other man? I hope I'm the only man in your life," he said teasing.

"Ryan, silly. How is your new case coming?"

"Pretty good, actually. I'm just about to wrap things up, maybe a couple more days. How's the book coming, making progress?" Sidney said sitting on the settee at the foot of the bed taking his shoes and socks off and pulling his shirttails out of his trousers.

"I'm pleased to report it's doing quite well, I may be finished sooner than I thought then we can start on the studio," she said taking the towel from her head and shaking out her hair.

"That's great Les, the sooner the better, mind if I watch the news?"

"No, go ahead, I'm going down and get a snack, you want anything? I'll have something to tell you when I return."

"More mysteries? I ate dinner about an hour ago so I'm good." Sidney called after Leslie as he heard her house shoes clicking on the wooden steps of the back staircase leading to the kitchen.

Lesley came back upstairs with a plate filled with crackers and cheese. Just as she entered the room, Sidney put his hand up for her to listen to the TV. She put the plate down on the table and sat next to him on the settee. The news was about Jonathon and his arrest, picture and all, then a picture of Rose Marie getting in her car and sobbing.

"Oh, poor Rose Marie, now was that necessary for that reporter to catch Jonathon's sister in such a vulnerable moment?" Leslie said.

"Why do I get the feeling you already know about this?" Sidney said reading the expression on Leslie's face.

"I feel so sorry for her. She came by here this afternoon. She was a basket case, just devastated after seeing Jonathon in jail. I tried to help her realize it wasn't her fault after all Jonathon is an adult and responsible for his adult actions."

"So, this is the family Annabelle was talking about? Did Rose Marie shed any light on the situation?" Sidney questioned.

"She's so distraught over the whole thing. I don't think she's gone beyond what she's able to deal with minute-by-minute, though"

"Well, Annabelle sure has her hands full with that family, the family trust, and trying not to get involved with Jonathon's case."

"Yes, and Sid, if she does get involved, how on earth will she get paid. Patrick was out trying to raise bail."

*****

"Did you see the news last night? What a horrible thing for Rose Marie and Patrick. I just could not believe my eyes. It was bad enough for them to smear the Bordeaux family's name but to show pictures of Rose Marie like that, well it was despicable," Sadie said sitting with Annabelle and Leslie having lunch.

"I agree, Rose Marie is taking this whole thing very hard," Leslie said looking at Annabelle. "She came to see me on her way home after visiting Jonathon in Jail. She's carrying the guilt of not spending more time with Jonathon and helping him with his faith. I told her the burden of guilt can weight one down. I encouraged her to take one step at a time and ask God to help. Personally, I don't know why Jonathon would do such a thing. It would be hard for me if it were my brother." Leslie said.

"We don't know the whole story yet, so it's hard to say what I would do if it were me," Sadie said.

"This is true. Without facts to go by we should not judge Jonathon, for all we know he had a good reason for what he did even if we can't imagine what that reason could be," Annabelle remarked looking into space as she tried to contemplate what could cause a person to commit such an act?

Chapter 5

When at last she looked up from the papers, Annabelle felt as though her neck was in a vice. Stretching and raising her shoulders to her ears she felt the release in her neck. As she moved her head back and forth she glanced at the clock on the wall.

"Half past eight, no wonder I'm starving," she said aloud to the empty room.

Stacking the papers, she put them back in the file and replaced it in the drawer. Locking the desk, she prepared to leave her office. With her back to the hall door, she reached for her cape, signature wide-brim hat, gloves and purse hanging on the coat rake.

Looking in the mirror as she adjusted her hat, she thought she saw movement in the hall through the opaque glass windows framing her office. Then she sensed something or someone behind her, taking a deep breath she turned slowly to find Jeffrey Bordeaux standing in the doorway.

"Oh, hello Jeffrey, you startled me. I didn't hear you come in. I really need to get a bell above that door. I'm just getting ready to leave. Can I do something for you?"

Jeffrey looked worn to a frazzle, the wrinkles on his face shown more prominently with the five o'clock shadow of his beard. He appeared smaller somehow, not the six feet he was but smaller, slumped over, tired.

Annabelle pulled up a chair and motioned for him to sit down. He didn't say a word, just looked at the floor like a little boy in trouble, then slowly he sat in the chair as she pulled another chair from across the room and sat down in front of him.

"Annabelle," Jeffrey said.

"Yes Jeffrey, what is it?"

"I'm so worried about Jonathon. I wanted to go see him, but I just couldn't bring myself to actually see him in jail, I guess I'm in denial. Did you see the news last night?" Annabelle nodded as Jeffrey continued. "Poor Rose Marie, I just don't know what to think or what to do. Patrick called and said Jonathon was released today. Did you know they put their home up for collateral to the bondsman?"

"Jeffrey, have you had dinner?"

He looked up at her surprised at her lack of concern.

"Jeffrey, I'm starving, and you probably need to eat too. We can't think straight on empty stomachs. So, what do you say we get a bite to eat and then we can talk,"

"You're right, I haven't eaten since breakfast and that was just a scone. Thank you, Annabelle. I appreciate your patience with me."

"No problem, now let's go find a place to have dinner," Annabelle said taking his arm with her glove clad hand and leading him to the door. She turned out the lights and locked the door.

They hailed a taxi and at Annabelle's suggestion went to Tujague's one of the oldest Restaurants in New Orleans on Decatur Street with its elegant yet leisurely atmosphere. The maître d' acknowledged Annabelle as a regular and showed them to their table where Jeffrey pulled out a chair for her helping with her cape then took the seat across the table facing her.

There was silence as they examined the menu. Decisions made on their choices for the meal and a wine selection they began small talk until the waiter set the salad in front of them and Annabelle bowed her head in prayer. Taking note, Jeffrey waited, then said Amen.

The evening was going well and with a good meal behind them, they finished eating their Bananas Foster then sipped coffee in the candlelight from the center of the table. Jeffrey was more relaxed, and he began to change the subject from his family to questions about Annabelle's life.

"I understand you have lived in the French Quarter all your life," Jeffrey commented.

"Yes, I grew up right here. My parents divorced, and I lived with my father until I went away to college. I inherited my father's practice," Annabelle said taking another sip of strong coffee. Not wanting to go any further into how her father's practice no longer existed she changed the subject. "Did you grow up here?"

"Yes, we grew up in a big typical New Orleans style house, well you probably know where it is since you knew my parents, God rest their souls. They would be very disappointed in Jonathon. In a way, I'm glad this all happened after they were gone."

"All indications are that Jonathon may have maneuvered the trust long before your parents died," Annabelle said.

"But they didn't know that, did they?"

"I doubt it. Jonathon was probably very clever with his control over the estate."

"That just doesn't sound like Jonathon, not that he isn't smart but to maneuver the trust like that... Well, that would take a lot of guts... I...," he said as he stared into space.

Annabelle watched as Jeffrey began to mull things over in his mind. As the lack of conversation surrounded them, she took note of how handsome Jeffrey was at around, guessing his age to be forty, maybe mid-forties. He must be a workaholic like me, she thought, because as far as she knew he had never married. A very successful businessman with several employees, he lived in an exclusive neighborhood in a historic house and on the surface seemed to be happy with his life until now as he dealt with the Bordeaux family crisis. Annabelle continued to contemplate what went on in Jeffrey's world. Jeffrey's stare turned to recognition as he became aware her eyes were fixed on him.

"Sorry, habit you know of being an attorney, sizing up your opponent," Annabelle said a little embarrassed.

"Do you consider me your opponent?" Jeffrey said with a frown.

"No, that's just an expression," again feeling embarrassed.

"I've enjoyed this evening with you Annabelle, I don't socialize much unless it's with clients and that becomes superficial at best, because I find it hard to have intelligent conversations with some people. It's refreshing to talk with someone without explaining everything I say. Sometimes, I feel like I'm on another planet from the people around me. But I don't feel that way around you.

You're a very savvy lady with a successful career and I certainly admire that about you."

"Wow, that's the most compliments a person can take in one sitting, thank you, I think. I don't want to disappoint you, but I'm pretty down to earth. I only get brainy when I talk lawyer stuff," she said with a smile.

Jeffrey burst out laughing, so hard he almost spilt his coffee. He leaned back in his chair and shook his head.

"Not only are you brainy but you have a great sense of humor." Then with a serious look, he asked, "Annabelle, your name is different from your father's, are you married?"

"I was! My husband was murdered," she said matter of fact.

"Murdered?" he remarked in surprise.

"Yes, it's a long story for another time but for now as much as I hate to I'm a working girl and I really must call it a night as I have an early meeting in the morning. I'm glad we had this time to get better acquainted, and Jeffrey I've also enjoyed this evening," she told him as he helped her from her seat.

"Thank you, Jeffrey," she said taking note of the way he helped her with her cape and then guided her through the tables with a familiar feeling as he put his hand on her back until they reached the door to the outside.

Pulling her cape tight around her shoulders in the brisk evening air as she and Jeffrey stood on the sidewalk outside the restaurant waiting to flag down a taxi, she could not help but notice how attractive he was in the glow of the street lantern. As the taxi pulled to the curb Jeffrey offered to ride with her to her place in the French Quarter, but she graciously declined, assuring him she would be fine. He held the door as she got in, then they waved goodbye.

Watching as Jeffrey's silhouette faded into the night, Annabelle realized how very long it had been since she had experienced a man's attention and she felt herself wanting more. Leaning her head back, she closed her eyes and taking a deep breath; she dared to imagine what a relationship with Jeffrey would bring to her life now and possibly in the future. Admitting to herself she could actually move on without her late husband Dean was frightening but on the other hand, she felt excited that she could even entertain the idea of dating since that had not happened in the many years since his death.

As the wind whipped around the corner of the restaurant, Jeffrey turned his back against it and watched as Annabelle's taxi pulled away from the curb heading for the French Quarter. He thought how pleasant the evening had been, no business, just two people enjoying each other's company and how relaxed he felt.

He didn't find time to go on real dates any more, just work-related gatherings and occasionally a business acquaintance needing an escort, but it had been months since he pursued a woman for a date. Loneliness was not something he admitted to often, because he filled his life with business nearly twenty-four hours a day, seven days a week. And, when he was not working, he volunteered for everything that came along. However, tonight made him realize he was indeed lonely, lonely for companionship, and what better companion would he find than Annabelle. She was smart, good company, had a good sense of humor not to mention easy on the eyes. *Let me see*, he calculated, *she must be in her thirties or maybe early forties depending on how long she was married. Murder? I really don't remember that and surely, I would've seen it in the paper*, he pondered.

Entering his New Olean's style uptown shotgun home, he tossed his keys in the tray on the table in the entryway. Walking down the hall, he thought how much he liked this house. His sister, Katrina Louise found it for him when she first got her broker's license. It was the only house he looked at because it was perfect for him, a two-story, not too big, but big enough, with a perfect-sized backyard and patio for entertaining with very little grass to mow.

He took his sports coat off and hung it on a hanger in the hall closet, before heading for his study. He sat at his desk and began to search the internet for a Robicheaux in New Orleans and there it was, 'Prominent Local Attorney's Husband found Dead of Apparent Suicide,' but she said murder, he thought scrolling down the screen where he found another headline, 'Dean Robicheaux Local Accountant Apparent Suicide Ruled Murder.' Additional information in the article gave Jeffrey more insight than he bargained for including the involvement of Sidney and Leslie Rye, good friends of his sister and her husband. He began to hope that maybe Jonathon could also be innocent of the charges against him and once the truth came out they could clear his name of all wrongdoing. He turned the light out and stared into the darkness contemplating what would happen to Jonathon if he was proven guilty.

Chapter **6**

Leslie had not seen Annabelle in a few days and because her book was moving along faster than expected, she buried herself in the pages hoping for a completion soon. Typing away as fast as her brain would allow, she didn't notice when Annabelle walked across the court yard and opened the cottage door.

"Leslie?" Annabelle said for the third time, raising her voice.

"Oh, you startled me, how long have you been there?"

"Not long but it's a good thing the gate is locked. You would never know if anyone came back here."

"Sorry, I'm on a roll, I may be finished sooner than I thought. I'm sending three more chapters to the editor today, I just hope there isn't a lot of rewrite," Leslie said reluctantly as she stopped typing. Sitting back in the chair, she looked up at Annabelle.

"You look like the cat that swallowed the canary, what's up?"

"I'm just marinating some thoughts. How much do you know about Rose Marie's brother Jeffrey?" Annabelle said.

"Not much, he's a successful business man, younger than Rose Marie, good looking. Why?"

"I kind of, sort of had a date with him, well maybe not a date more like a casual dinner."

"What? Do tell me more," Leslie said teasing, flashing a grin at her friend.

Pulling up a chair, Annabelle told her about the night she and Jeffrey had dinner and how she had not been able to stop thinking about him since.

"I see, thus the thought marinating?"

"In some ways, it's exciting to think I could ever have another love in my life, but then I begin to feel guilty, like I'm cheating on Dean. It's very confusing, because I never thought I could love anyone other than Dean and now I'm actually thinking about another man in…well you know a romantic way."

"Annabelle, I think it is wonderful. I'm so happy for you and I didn't know Dean but I would imagine he would be happy for you too."

"You really think so Leslie?"

"Yes, I do, you deserve a life full of love and happiness. Annabelle, you're still young and quite beautiful, so why not go for it? Do you think Jeffrey feels the same way you do?"

"Oh, Leslie, he was so attentive just like Dean always was, a real gentleman, so polite. I hope he feels the same way. I must not get my hopes up. I know he saw the wedding ring that I cannot part with, let alone take it off my finger. So, when he asked me why I had a different name from my father, well, I just told him my husband was murdered and he was truly shocked."

"Well, I guess so, did you explain, or did you just drop the bomb shell on him and move on, like you usually do?" Lesley said shaking her head in disapproval.

"It was getting late and I just didn't want to go into the whole thing right then, I didn't want to end the evening on a negative note."

"So, you think telling him Dean was murdered was a positive note?" Leslie said stifling the urge to laugh.

"Probably not. But, oh well, I probably blew it." Annabelle said feeling a sadness.

"Wait and see he may be curious enough to call for another 'social' date," Lesley said two fingers in the air to show quotation marks. "In the meantime, I'm starving, let's have lunch."

"But, I interrupted you, and I'm sorry, since you said you were on a roll. I guess that's writer talk."

"Don't be silly we have to eat. So, come on. The book will wait. Anyway, I want to hear more about this 'social date.'" Leslie said pushing Annabelle out the door.

*****

Sitting across from each other, Leslie leaned forward to hear more clearly what Annabelle described as a wonderful evening with a handsome man she thought, for the first time in a long time, she could have feelings for.

"But the problem is, I can't get involved with Jeffrey if I represent the family or even Jonathan because it would be a conflict of interest. So, even if I would like the relationship to continue, it can't, due to the circumstance. Oh, Leslie I'm really jumping ahead of myself. I don't know if he even feels the same way I do," Annabelle said shaking her head.

"Now Annabelle, I'm sure it will work out somehow, you'll just need to have faith and trust in God. If this is the man He has chosen for you then the details will work out. We'll just pray that God will show the way,"

Chapter 7

The experience was unpleasant, humiliating and sobering. At first, survival was almost unattainable as Jonathon found himself surrounded by criminals on every level. Humans hurting other humans through violence and thievery. Thoughts of judgment brought him face to face with his own behavior. Seeing Rose Marie was the hardest thing yet, knowing her disappointment in him nearly brought him to tears especially when she tried so hard to make sense of everything that was happening. He was also having trouble understanding the situation. He desperately wanted to confide in someone, tell the whole story from beginning to end, but not knowing how the law worked, he hesitated to confide in anyone but a lawyer, and he wanted Annabelle to be that Lawyer.

Sitting in the conference room across the table from Jonathon, Annabelle told him it could be a conflict of interest to represent him and the family.

"Your family has not hired me. The only reason I'm involved is that my dad drew up the family trust and his name was on the record at the bank as their attorney. The branch manager at the bank is a friend of mine, and she called me when they found all of the discrepancies. I agreed to meet with your family to give them the news."

"Annabelle, I'm really in trouble here and you're the only one I feel comfortable with representing me."

"Since your family has not hired me to represent them and because you have no means to pay my fee, I will ask the court to appoint me as your attorney."

"How will you get paid?"

"Don't worry Jonathon, I'll worry about that."

"Am I going to get out of here after the hearing?"

"Bail has been set and posted so you'll be released soon."

*****

With his bail posted, Jonathon approached Patrick who was waiting at the desk. When he saw Jonathon, the relief was evident in them both as the two men shook hands and walked out of the building. Patrick drove Jonathon to his condominium as they shared small talk about the weather, a recent sports event and never once did the subject come up about the charges against Jonathon. Patrick offered to stay with him, but Jonathon insisted he wanted to be alone to take a real shower, eat a decent meal and sleep in his own bed. So, Patrick left him at the gate to the courtyard of his condominium.

Jonathon unlocked the gate and went through the familiar courtyard up the stairs as if nothing had happened. He walked through the door closing it behind him, leaned back against it and shook his head in disbelief. How had he allowed such a thing to happen? Was he in denial knowing all along that eventually, something would stop the whole thing? His thoughts rambled on for a while as he showered and then put on clothes from his closet. The jail attire was humiliating and degrading, and he was glad to have a choice in his own clothes. After dressing, he went downstairs and took a frozen dinner out of the freezer and put it in the microwave. He surmised that the TV dinner was much better than jail food. The microwave buzzed, but deep in thought, he ignored it. He went to the den and sat in his oversized leather chair until the room became darkened as the sun set.

The ringing woke him from a sound sleep, reaching for the phone receiver he hesitated then said "Hello"

"Jonathon are you alright? Did I wake you?"

"What time is it?" he said recognizing his sister's voice

"Eight."

"Morning or night?"

"Night, Jonathon, it's eight in the evening," Rose Marie said.

"Yeah, I'm alright just sleep deprived I guess," Jonathon said staying in his chair as thoughts of sleeping where hardened criminals slept came rushing back causing his heart rate to increase.

"Did you eat dinner?"

"I think so.… I don't really remember…. Don't worry sis I'm okay. I just need some time to think things through and figure out where to go from here."

"Jonathon… If there is anything we can do, please let us know."

"You and Patrick have done more than your share already and I do appreciate it especially under the circumstances. I hope someday you can forgive me," and with that said, he said good-bye and hung up the phone.

Hunger pains gnawed at him until he finally rose from his chair, entering the kitchen, he remembered the TV dinner in the microwave. Tossing it in the trash, he decided to clean up and go out to eat.

He was acutely aware of the freedom he had to drive a car, go to a restaurant, order from a menu, and make decisions about simple things like what to wear, what to listen to on the radio or watch on TV. These thoughts brought him back to the reality of his situation. Those freedoms could be taken away if he were found guilty of his crime and that's why he needed Annabelle.

Soon he was at his favorite restaurant, Tujague on Decatur facing the French Market. After parking the car down the street, he walked on the sidewalk toward the door when suddenly as he looked in the window, he saw his brother Jeffrey and Annabelle sitting at a table in candlelight laughing and seemingly enjoying each other's company. He turned around and went back to his car. As he pulled out of the parking space, he saw the two of them come out of the building and hail a cab. He hoped that they didn't see him as he passed them on the roadway. Unnerved by the scene he had just witnessed, he set out to find a drive-through for his dinner.

Back at home, he finalized his thoughts of Annabelle and Jeffrey. Seeing them together put his future in jeopardy. It was bad enough when it was him against the family but not him against Annabelle's romantic involvement with his brother. *Why had he not known that Jeffrey and Annabelle were an item, no wonder she hesitated to accept his case.* He wanted to talk to Annabelle and ask her how long she had been seeing his brother but he thought better of that idea and decided to ask her instead to recommend another lawyer.

Chapter **8**

Katrina Louise tried to keep her mind on the job as she took clients, a middle-aged professional couple, through a sizeable mid-century revival in the garden district. Pointing out the high ceilings and stucco walls, she kept pace with the couple as they went from room to room. The house had been vacant for several months and needed some work. However, the price was right, and she needed this sale. She had bit off a big mortgage on a house down the street when it came on the market a couple of months before, and the payments were eating her lunch as they say.

This sale would pay several months payments and give her the breather she needed on her budget. Although financially independent, she had hoped to invest her portion of the estate in another garden district property, flipping it to make a profit. Katrina Louise was disappointed in Jonathon, but not devastated by the loss of her inheritance. She loved her career and was determined to build her nest egg with her earnings for retirement in a few years.

A failed marriage in her twenties, she vowed never to depend on a man financially again. When she got her broker's license, her first sale was to her brother Jeffrey. That commission gave her the opportunity to open her own brokerage and take on three more realtors increasing the listings for the brokerage and freeing her up to handle more sales, which was her forte. She could smell a sale a mile away, and closure was the thing that truly excited her as she figured the commission in her head with each closing word.

There were men in her life, mostly acquaintances, nothing serious because she never let it go that far. A trail of brokenhearted rejections followed her as she discarded each male without so much as a "so long." It just was not worth the time and effort; she had other more important things to occupy her life and making money was her top priority.

Whatever was going on with Jonathon, she wondered if she would have helped him financially if he had come to her, the answer was clear, *no she wouldn't have, well maybe if it had been life or death.*

"This house checks all of the boxes on your list including the price," she said giving the final pitch that sealed the deal as she gave the history of the old house right down to the iron cornstalk fence that surrounded the once immaculate gardens now in dire need of some TLC.

"Miss Bordeaux, are you any relations to that Jonathon Bordeaux charged with embezzlement?"

"Yes, but let's not let that interfere with you getting this house as I know it is right for you," Katrina Louis said without skipping a beat.

"You're right, we love it," they told her.

"Well then, let's go back to the office and write up an offer," Katrina Louise said. "I'll call ahead and make sure that everything is ready when we get there. Oh, you're just going to love this place, I just know you will."

As she was talking to the office, she received another call on her cell, looking at the number she realized it was Jeffrey. *I'll call him back later; this is not the time to chat about Jonathon,* she said to herself taking a deep breath already irritated at the question from her clients about her relationship with someone who would embezzle.

Chapter *9*

Annabelle sat in her office trying to wade through the paperwork but found it increasingly difficult as her thoughts wandered back to the other night with Jeffrey. She had not been able to put the evening out of her mind for days. Deep in thought, it took a couple of rings before she answered.

"Hello"

"Mrs. Robicheaux, this is Bryce with the DA's office. Have you talked to Jonathon Bordeaux in the last few days? We have been unable to locate him and thought you might have had contact with him."

"What do you mean? Do you think he has skipped bail?"

"It sure looks that way, we had a guy checking on him just in case, and he seems to have flown the coop."

"I wouldn't know where to begin to look for him, his condo, boat, I think he sold his clock business months ago. I'm sorry I don't think I can help you."

"We haven't located his boat either we think he may have left in it to God only knows where. Any clues?"

"Not really, I didn't even know he had a boat until this all came about, how far could he get, it's a sailboat, surely, he wouldn't set out to sea from the gulf," she said concerned.

"Desperate people seek desperate measures when faced with a jail sentence."

"If in fact, that's what he's doing, I hope he reconsiders for his sake. This will only make matters worse," Annabelle told the DA.

"I'll keep you informed, and if you come up with anything, we sure could use some help on this."

"Thank you, Bryce," she said thinking about the bail money that Patrick and Rose Marie put up and wondered if any of the siblings knew of his whereabouts. *I have to call Leslie and Sidney; they will not believe this. I don't believe it myself. Jonathon must have known the outcome of his trial would be guilty as charged and decided to make a run for it,* she thought.

*****

Rose Marie put the receiver of the phone down then stared out the window of her home office. Their backyard, manicured by Patrick's skillful hands put a brief smile on her face. Then a shiver came over her as she remembered they had used their house for Jonathon's bail. She pushed the feeling aside knowing her brother wouldn't do anything to jeopardize their home.

She had just broken the news of Jonathon's release with her daughter Lisa, their oldest child and mother of their two grandchildren. Lisa seemed calm enough as her mother explained, almost too calm, Rose Marie thought not moving from her view of the backyard. She had asked Lisa to break the news to her brothers. Thinking back on the conversation, she wished she had not put that burden on her daughter. Picking the receiver back up she dialed the number only to hear a busy signal. Assuming Lisa was on the phone with one of her brothers, she hung up.

"Rose Marie, I'm going to go to the market and get something to grill for dinner tonight, okay with you, hon?" Patrick said behind her chair massaging her shoulders. "You okay, honey?" he said when she didn't answer him.

"I guess, I just don't know what has happened to my family Patrick, they are all on a collision course, they need God in their life, and I don't know how to make that happen."

"Sweetheart, you can't make them do what they don't want to do. We all make our own choices in life. I'm just glad your choice was spending your life with me. I love you Rose Marie and it hurts me to see you in so much pain. We can only do our best, you and I, and we have so many things to be grateful for, our kids and grandkids for one and the fact that God put us together. We will survive this, you know," Patrick said kissing her on her forehead before leaving the room.

*****

Patrick examined the fish counter looking for the freshest tuna steaks when someone spoke to him from behind, turning he found himself face to face with Derik, a social acquaintance, and the local newspaper editor.

"Hello Patrick, that tuna looks good, getting ready to grill maybe?"

"Thinking about it. How've you been Derik?" Patrick said avoiding eye contact, still looking over the fish in front of him.

"Pretty good, pretty good," he repeated with a tone that made Patrick a little weary as he wondered what Derik's next question would be.

"Well, I think this will do," Patrick said selecting the fish he wanted, "good to see you again Derik, say hello to your wife for me," he said walking away.

"Patrick?"

"Yes," he said slowly turning to face him.

"We have a guy in the DA office and the word is that Jonathon can't be found anywhere, and he may have jumped bail. I just thought that you might want to contribute something, since it'll hit the front page tomorrow."

Patrick stared blankly at Derik not believing what he was telling him, trying to form his words appropriately, he thought for a minute before answering.

"Derik, this is a family matter that I don't feel free to discuss with you, I'm sure you can understand," Patrick said.

"I'm sorry Patrick,"

"You're just doing your job, Derik," Patrick said turning and heading for the checkout stand. Back in his car, he took out his cell phone and dialed Annabelle's number.

"Hello."

Patrick told her of his encounter with Derik and asked her if she knew what was going on.

"Yes, I got a call from the DA's office. I didn't call any of you because I thought they could find him. I just wanted to give him time."

"Do you think he's on the run?"

"I'm assuming he is, his boat is missing." Annabelle said

"What boat, he didn't have a boat, did he?"

"Yes, a pretty good size sailboat, big enough to get him away from here. Patrick since the police are working on this without any luck, you may want to consider hiring Sidney, he's really good at what he does, and he will be as discreet as possible. Now if it hits the papers tomorrow, well, it will hamper his efforts, but I have the utmost confidence in Sidney, if anyone can find him Sidney can."

"I guess the others better be told before they read it in the paper," Patrick said.

"I'll take care of that right now. Tell Rose Marie to keep the faith. I'm praying for all of you, Patrick."

"Thank you, Annabelle, call me if anything changes. I want to know any new developments, we are the ones that posted bail, and we put up our home,"

"Patrick, if Jonathon does not return in time for the hearing in two weeks the arrangement for the bail will be called in."

"Thank you, Annabelle," he said before hanging up. Bowing his head, he tried to stay calm. God, we praise You and thank You for Your constant vigilance. Our hearts are broken Jesus over our brother Jonathon. We ask for his protection, and Jesus help my wife Rose Marie during this hard time. In your precious name, I pray. Amen.

Entering the kitchen from the back door, he put the tuna steaks in the refrigerator then went looking for Rose Marie. He found her right where he left her in her office upstairs.

"So, what are we having for dinner?" she asked. Then noticing the look on his face, she put her pen down and asked, "what is it, Patrick?"

After explaining to his wife what he had learned, and the call to Annabelle, he took her in his arms and held her as she sobbed. A few minutes later, she pushed back from him as he handed her some tissues from her desk. Wiping her eyes, she told him how she had always had a feeling that Jonathon wouldn't serve his sentence even if arrested.

"I don't know why I feel that way Patrick, I just do. I hope Jonathon is all right. Do you think Sidney will be able to find him?"

"Annabelle seems to be confident he will. She says he's excellent at investigation and that's why she wants us to hire him. She said the court would probably give the detectives 14 days to find him before revoking the bail money."

"But if the police can't find him…," Rose Marie started.

"Shhh, don't second guess this honey, just trust that someone will find him," he assured her. "We need to let God know we trust Him. Scripture says, *'be anxious for nothing, but in everything by prayer and supplication, with thanksgiving, let your requests be made known to God.'* Let's ask God to protect him and bring him back safe."

Chapter **10**

After feeding Ryan, she took him off for his bath and put him into his pajamas. Reading to him from *Winnie the Pooh,* she watched as he pointed to the pictures and tried to say the words that go with them. She helped him along, pleased with his effort and hoped Sidney would be home soon to see his son trying to read. The thought no sooner left her mind than Sidney appeared at the nursery door with a wide grin of pride on his face.

"That's my boy, Ryan, you're really learning fast. Thank you, Leslie, for reading to him, I think he understands."

Putting the book down, they put Ryan to bed and kissed him goodnight. Then, after lights out, they turned on the monitor and the nightlight.

"Goodnight sweet boy, we'll see you in the morning," Leslie said following Sidney out of the room. Arm and arm they headed down the hall to the stairs. In the kitchen, Leslie asked if he was hungry.

"Yeah, I'm starved, how about a steak? I'll do the steak if you'll do the salad, and maybe we can split a baked potato."

"Sounds good, I'll get started," Leslie said turning on the facet to wash her hands.

Her cell phone started ringing. "Can you get that honey? My hands are wet?"

"Hello," Sidney said with the phone between his shoulder and chin while retrieving steaks from the refrigerator. "Hi Annabelle, what's up?... No, we're just starting dinner, why?"

Annabelle told him she had some things to talk to him about then asked if she could come over later.

"Why don't you come on over now?" he said looking at Leslie for approval. Leslie nodded. "No problem. I'm grilling steaks and we have enough. Les is going to throw some potatoes on and prepare a salad. How does that sound?... Alright then see you soon."

"What's going on?" Leslie asked washing her hands.

"She didn't say, just that she wanted to talk to me about something, probably a case she wants help with."

"Then why did she call you on my cell?"

"Good question." Sidney said seasoning the steaks.

Leslie stopped tearing lettuce for the salad, and with a puzzled look on her face, she said. "Sid, I bet it has something to do with Jonathon," then turning back to the salad, she began chopping scallions as she pondered the possibility that this was precisely the reason why Annabelle had called.

The table set and the potatoes almost done, Leslie lit the candles in the center of the table and asked Annabelle who had just arrived if she would like a glass of wine.

"Thanks Leslie, I would love some. It looks so nice in here, I love this house and I love what you have done with it. It feels like home."

"You're welcome and thank you, we love it too, it's been a lot of hard work, but the results are very satisfying," Lesley said putting the salad on the table. "What kind of dressing suits your fancy?"

"Oil and Vinegar is fine with me."

"Then you won't mind if I put it in the salad now, that's the way we like it, if that's okay," Lesley said taking the bowl back to the kitchen.

Annabelle followed her and watched as she tossed the dressing in the salad, then turning to Sidney she asked, "How's business, are you real busy?"

"Steady. Can always use more business, got to keep this place up you know and bring home the bacon for my family. Why? You have something in mind?"

"We'll talk over dinner."

Annabelle told them about the DA's call, and she suspected that Jonathon was on the lamb. "Told you it would make a good book Leslie, so Sidney will you talk to Patrick and see if he will hire you to find Jonathon?" she said looking at Sidney.

"I'm just as curious as you are Annabelle, but let's be practical, we do need to make a living, after all, I'm not sure where my fee will come from especially since Patrick put up the bail money. Is Patrick going to foot your fee also? If you can take Jonathon's case, I don't want you spending money hiring me if you're not getting paid." Sidney told her.

"Now Mr. Worry Wart, don't you worry about little ole me, I'll manage. I'm concerned about this family and of course Jonathon. From all indications, it just isn't like him. It's totally out of character, so what's really going on? Don't you feel it Sidney, you know that nagging feeling we get when faced with a mystery?"

"I must admit it has piqued my interest. Well, if you're sure you want me to take this on, have Patrick call me. But, make a decision soon on representing Jonathon. You may be his only chance. I'll let you know how it goes with Patrick."

The next morning after much consideration and urging from Annabelle, Patrick called Sidney, and they agreed to meet for coffee.

"Good morning, Patrick," Sidney said standing up from his chair shaking Patrick's hand. They both sat down, and Patrick began telling Sidney about not being able to locate Jonathon. He also explained the dilemma Annabelle had with representing Jonathon. Even though this information was not news to him, Sidney listened without interruption to determine Patrick's take on it.

"It'll be in our best interest to have you look for him, and as you say, if Annabelle is allowed to represent him then you can switch over to her team."

They discussed pay arrangements and Sidney accepted the case assuring Patrick he would do his best to find Jonathan before the bond expired.

Chapter **11**

Walking on the deck of the marina Sidney examined the slip where Jonathon kept his boat moored, kneeling down on one knee, he leaned over the edge where rope fragments hung loose, the rope was cut below the knot tied to the cleat. There were fragments of paint chips attached to the side of the slip as if the boat had rammed it hard.

"Someone was in a big hurry to leave," Sidney said aloud to no one since he was the only one on the deck. He stood looking out at the calm water in the Gulf of Mexico. The past few days, probably a week now, the weather had been mild, calm winds, no rain, *how far could one get in a decent size boat in weather like that? I would imagine pretty far,* he thought.

"How long would it take to get out of the gulf and reach the open waters, like say headed for the Islands?" Sidney asked the salty looking character in the supply shack.

"I don't know. It would depend on the size of the boat and of course the weather, why?" the seedy toothless guy with a beard and fishing hat answered.

"Do you know the owner of the boat in slip 5, you know the big sailboat, red white and blue paint?"

"You mean the B. J.? Sure, I know Jon and that lady friend of his, they come out here often, why?"

"Have you seen them in the last few days, say within the last week?" Sidney asked hiding his surprise at Jonathon having a lady friend.

"I saw him, he was loading the B.J., said he would be out for a few days and needed supplies, is there a problem?"

"His family is worried about him, here is my card would you give me a call if you see him again, I would really appreciate it, Nate is it, right?" he said noticing the name on his shirt.

"Yeah Mr. Rye, Nate," he said looking at the card, "the lady too?"

"Describe the lady." Sidney said curiously.

"Late fifties, maybe older, tall, dark hair, somewhat a looker for her age, dressed kind of uppity, you know like she owned the world, she sure was in charge of Jon, if you know what I mean."

"Yeah, thanks Nate, let me know, okay?'

Chapter **12**

Their early marriage was full of extravagant trips and lavish parties until they decided to settle down and raise a family. For months, they tried to get pregnant; then when tested they found out that Robert had a lower than low sperm count. They tried everything even going to their priest to intervene with God, but when nothing happened, they finally gave up.

Robert wouldn't hear of adoption because the child wouldn't have his bloodline. So, the downhill spiral began. Robert was in denial about his medical condition and blamed it all on Sandy. As years went on, Sandy became bitter, syndical and outspoken. Her language would put a sailor to shame and her hardness shown like a beacon on her face. Once a good-looking woman, now her leather skin, from too much sun, and the frown painted on her face made her look way beyond her years. Unknown to the Bordeaux family, she had once attempted suicide by downing a bottle of pills.

"Oh no you don't, you're not leaving me to face this by myself," she remembered Robert yelling at her as he dragged her around the room then filled her full of some awful stuff that made her vomit. After that, he locked up her pills, doling them out one by one.

As they were leaving the restaurant, they had a heated discussion about Jonathon skipping bail.

"Where do you suppose he is, Robert? I just want to tell him face to face…," Sandy said getting in the car, and barely shutting the door before Robert stepped on the gas throwing her back against the seat.

"Tell him what? It won't bring back the money, the jewelry, the paintings, the house or anything, it is all gone, and in case you forgot it was my money, not yours, this was Bordeaux money," Robert said turning onto the highway headed out of town. "I'm just lucky I didn't help put up bail money as if I would ever do anything to help my big brother."

"Where are you going, aren't we going to try and find him?" Sandy said, desperate.

"You haven't heard a word I said, and besides my heart won't take much more today, so unless you want both of us to die in a car crash I suggest you shut up."

When things started going bad between them, Robert took Sandy's name off the checking account, the house, and even her car. Every payday he put a large percentage of his check in another account she knew nothing about, then gave her an allowance. He knew she wanted to leave him but without funds, she would have a hard time doing it. He kept up appearances of a somewhat functional marriage but managed to keep a few relationships on the side without Sandy suspecting anything. He had her right where he wanted her, under his thumb. When the time was right, he planned to walk out the front door and never look back.

However, lately he was experiencing some chest pain that had him concerned. So, without anyone aware, he went to a cardiologist and had his heart checked out. The doctor put him on some pills for his blood pressure and irregular heart beat and told him to try to eliminate some of the stress in his life.

"Fat chance of that happening," he told the doctor. "My life is 24-7 stress, and there is not much I can do about it."

"Robert if you're so worried about your heart, why don't you go see a doctor?" Sandy said as they drove toward Shreveport where they lived.

"Mind your own business."

"Well, you're always complaining and talking about having a heart attack, I just think you should check it out," Sandy said trying to sound sympathetic.

"You sound like you really care, and Sandy we know that isn't true. So, why the concern?" Robert asked glancing over at her.

"Forget it, Robert, do what you want, I'm just tired of your constant complaining," she said turning away from him and watching the scenery go by out the car window.

Chapter **13**

Her fingers were flying over the keys as her ideas flowed like the smooth run of molten lava, exciting and intriguing, she loved it when the words came so fast. Four hours had passed without a break when suddenly her shoulders, tense from the strain, began to tighten, her neck was stiff, and the pain in her lower back cried out to her for a break.

The events over the past few days had inspired her to finish this book, so she could start another right away before the creative juices ran dry. Hands to her side she began to make fists, opening and closing, working the circulations back into her fingers. All the while reading over the copy, *yes, yes that's exactly what I wanted,* she said to herself as she leaned back in her chair and looked out over the courtyard.

What a beautiful day, I wonder if Jonathon's day is beautiful, she thought with sorrow in her heart. *Father, please protect him,* she prayed thinking of his family especially Rose Marie. Then after dialing the number, she heard Rose Marie's voice on the other end of the line, distant, anxious, and obviously waiting for news.

"Rose Marie, it's Leslie, how are you doing?"

"Hello Leslie, okay I guess, just hoping for some news. Have you heard anything?"

"No, and I'm sure you'll be the first to know if there is any news. Is there anything I can do for you?"

"No, I just want to keep the line free for any news, you understand," she said.

"Sure, call if you hear anything."

Leslie sat staring out the windows when a thought hit her and dialing Sid's cell she waited listening to each ring, tapping her fingers on the desk.

When his voice mail came on, she told him to call her. Not wanting to scare him, she added, "about Jonathon."

*****

Sidney was backtracking from his talk with Nate at the dock trying to find some information on the woman seen with Jonathon. So far, it had been a dead end, about the woman anyway but he was following a lead about where the two of them may have stayed up the coast toward Mississippi. He almost forgot that Leslie had left a message earlier as he quickly pushed her speed dial: number one.

"Les, sorry I'm just now getting back to you, what's up?"

"That's okay, I almost forgot, let's see, why did I call? Oh yeah, I was just thinking that Jonathon may not have enough experience to navigate open waters, perhaps he's staying close in and heading along the coast either toward Florida or maybe Mexico. My bet would be Mexico."

"I thought of that, but the police have an APB out on him and the boat so if that were the case surely someone would spot him in a big red, white and blue cruiser with a big B. J. plastered on the side. I'm following a lead right now where he and his lady friend may have stayed up the coast toward Mississippi." Sid said.

"Lady Friend? Wow, the plot thickens, how did you know he had a lady friend?"

"My good friend Nate on the dock even gave me a description."

"Hey, maybe it's her initials on the boat," Les said enthusiastically.

"That's a thought, maybe he named the boat after her. Good idea, partner."

"I wonder why all the secrecy, I'm sure Rose Marie doesn't know anything about a lady friend and neither does Annabelle. Do you suppose the police know anything?" Leslie pondered.

"Don't think so, nobody has mentioned her if they are aware of her existence, but I think that's the clue to this whole thing, you know, the embezzled money and all."

"Yeah, could be, maybe she's the wife of a mobster or something," Leslie said laughing.

"There you go again with those wild ideas, save it for those books you write. I'll keep in touch, and I'll talk to you later. I may be late for supper, keep a candle in the window. I love you," Sidney said before hanging up.

Looking at the napkin with the scrawled picture of a map the bartender a few blocks back had given him, he slowed down. He turned into the circular drive and leaned over the dashboard to find the name of the hotel. He surmised he was indeed in the right place, although quite taken aback by the luxury of the surrounding area looking out over the gulf.

Well, this isn't exactly a dive, or a cheap meeting place for a secret lovers' rendezvous, this is high priced accommodations, he thought as he parked across from the entrance, nose out, as was his custom, for a quick getaway if needed.

"Hello, my name is Sidney Rye, here's my card," he said handing the card to the man behind the counter.

"What can I do for you Mr. Rye?"

"Do you recognize this man?" said Sid, showing him a picture of Jonathon.

"Maybe, is his wife looking for him?"

"Actually, his wife died a couple of years ago; he's missing. So, have you seen him? He may have been with a woman, dark hair, tall, good looking and fancy dresser."

"Yeah, I've seen them, they stay here off and on,"

"Have they stayed here lately, like in the last week or so?" Sid asked, handing the informant a twenty.

"No sir they haven't been here for over a month, at least not when I'm on duty. Let me check the computer, let's see Williams was the name they gave if I remember right, yeah here it is about two weeks ago, room 308."

Sidney thanked him and asked to speak to the housekeeper that was on duty when they stayed in room 308 two weeks ago. He got on the elevator, went to the third floor, and showed the picture to Sonia, the housekeeper. She had little to add except she thought they were newlyweds because they stayed to themselves in their room. He left word for the desk clerk and the housekeeper to call him the minute they saw either one of them or remembered anything that might be of help.

Knowing his run-away couple would have to show ID when checking in to any reputable hotel, Sidney went about checking contacts to see where they had the fake IDs made and how long ago the couple found the need to have documents to hide their identity. *What were these two up to anyway?* He thought back in the car. Sitting there long enough to get his thoughts together, he made some calls, jotted down some notes then turned toward the coastal highway. Driving along the gulf, he tried to imagine sailing a boat through the fierce waves slapping against the shore. Closer to New Orleans, sandy beaches began to fill with people, reminding Sidney of the long walks he and Leslie would take on the beach before they had Ryan and got too busy. *We'll have to change that.* He thought.

*****

Sunday morning found the small group of believers gathered at the Rye house. By this time, the members of the group had read the papers and knew the story behind Jonathon's disappearance. They all offered support and prayers for Rose Marie and Patrick who had come early to see if there were any new developments Sidney could share with them. Sidney was not anxious to share anything at this point until verification, so his answer was simple and direct. He told them no news was good news, and he was still following leads.

"Hello Sadie, Joe," Leslie said hugging Sadie. "Come on in, did Annabelle come with you?"

"Yes, she is on the phone. She'll be in shortly," Joe said.

Greeting the rest of the group in the living room, Sadie and Joe found a seat near Rose Marie and Patrick. Sadie gave Rose Marie a hug while Joe shook hands with Patrick. Everyone present, the meeting was about to begin when Annabelle came in and signaled to Sidney to come in the kitchen.

"What's up?"

"I just got off the phone with the DA's office, they had a tip that someone tied a boat to a dock up the coast, at the southernmost tip of Texas close to the Mexican border, that fits the description of Jonathon's boat," she said removing her hat and gloves.

"Well, Leslie was right, she thought they would head for Mexico," Sidney said

"They?"

"Yes, I haven't had a chance to tell you, there seems to be a woman involved in this mystery."

"Come on you two, we are ready to begin," Leslie said.

Annabelle looked at Sidney in surprise, "Well, that's a development," she whispered as she and Sidney joined the others.

Joe began with prayer and others joined in, first with a song, then with scripture readings and discussions. Rose Marie had noticed Annabelle and Sidney's conversation and wondered if there was any news. Patrick laid his hand over hers as Joe read from his bible *"lean not unto yourself, but lean on the Lord,"* he went on reading from scripture as tears came to Rose Marie's eyes. When he had finished reading, they all agreed with an *"Amen."* After a while, they took a break and Leslie with the help of some of the others served coffee, tea, and baguettes.

This gave Rose Marie a chance to corner Annabelle. "Have you heard something, I saw you talking with Sidney earlier, has something happened?"

"We don't know for sure, Rose Marie, they think they have spotted Jonathon's boat."

"Where? Is he alright?"

"Actually, they haven't located him, but they think the boat is docked up the coast close to the Mexican border," she told her.

"Mexico? Oh dear, he's running, isn't he? Oh, Annabelle what has happened to him? This is not the Jonathon I know; it's just not like him at all." Rose Marie said. "I would expect this of Robert, always impulsive, scheming, and secretive but not Jonathon, kind, sweet and giving, I just don't understand. I know we haven't been real close lately, and now I wonder if that's because he was ashamed of what he was doing, so ashamed he wanted to stay as far away from me as possible in order for me not to know something was terribly wrong. I try not to be judgmental, but I do live my convictions, and anyone that knows me knows that. So, I'm sure that's why he couldn't come to me, Annabelle, I just wish I could help him," she said with her head hung low.

"I understand, truly I do," Annabelle said remembering how hard it was to listen to people say her husband had committed suicide. When all along she knew, that was totally out of character and she was convinced he was murdered. "We'll get to the bottom of this Rose Marie, I promise."

The group had been studying the book of *John* and Sidney began teaching the lesson for the morning. It was obvious that Rose Marie and Patrick, try as they would, had other things on their mind especially after the news that Jonathon's boat may be docked in the Gulf close to Mexico.

After the meeting, as was their custom, the group stayed for a potluck lunch. Leslie brought the children in from the playroom where Daisy kept them occupied during the lesson. Ryan was excited to see Annabelle and reached his arms out to her.

"Come here you, big boy, you're growing up too fast Ryan, you'll be in school before we know it."

"Please don't even think about that, I can't stand the thought of him going off to school. I'm seriously thinking about homeschooling him." Leslie said kissing Ryan on the cheek. The other parents gave their sympathies and they all laughed remembering those same feelings when their children were babies.

Not long after the meal was finished, Rose Marie and Patrick said their goodbyes, left to return home where they could talk about what was going on, and tell the other siblings what they had learned.

Annabelle had stayed to help clean up and talk more to Sidney. Wiping the counter top with a cloth, Leslie turned to Annabelle.

"What do you make of the discovery of a women involved in this?"

"Not unusual, many men have done many evil things for the attention of a woman. However, to hear Rose Marie describe her brother it does seem strange that Jonathon has a lady friend no one knows about."

Chapter *14*

"**M**exico? Why's he in Mexico, can he do that, don't they have ways to make him come back? What's he going to do in Mexico?" A. J. yelled into the phone. "Did he take all our money to Mexico?"

"A. J. calm down, all we know is they think his boat was found near Mexico," Rose Marie said.

"Where did he get a boat?"

"He obviously bought it A. J.," Rose Marie said trying not to show her irritation with her sister's obvious lack of concentration.

"Really, so he bought a boat with our money, is that what you're saying?"

"Listen carefully," Rose Marie, said slowly, "the police must think the boat belongs to Jonathon, I don't know how they know that, maybe the license on the boat told them I don't know A. J., and all I know is what I've told you."

"Don't be mad, sis, I just can't believe this is happening to me, to all of us, you know what I mean? I really need that money, and now Jonathon has taken it with him to Mexico. Can't we find him and get it back?"

Rose Marie was well aware of her little sister's shortcomings. She listened for many years as her mother worried about A. J., the baby of the family. Her mother blamed herself for getting pregnant in her forties and for her daughter's condition saying her labor was hard and things went wrong, however, Rose Marie never quite understood what things went wrong. She was aware that A. J. got into drugs in high school and was in rehab a couple of times. Amazingly, A. J.'s kids didn't seem to have the same afflictions as their mother. How the judge awarded those children to their mother was beyond Rose Marie's comprehension although she did realize the Judge had a hard decision between their mother and two loser fathers.

The two older ones, a boy and a girl, now seventeen and eighteen, took care of the youngest, a ten-year-old girl. As their aunt, Rose Marie would check on them regularly, making sure they had all the necessities. Through the years she bought them new clothes, took them out to eat pizza and burgers when she would find them home alone. She talked to A. J. many times about taking care of her kids and offered to raise them, but A. J. was terrified that the child support payments would stop, and she would have to go to work.

At one point, Rose Marie threatened to turn her in to the court if she didn't pay closer attention to her children. A. J. moved and changed her phone number so Rose Marie could not find them, but after searching for months in all the schools in the parishes in New Orleans, she finally found them through a priest in Breaux Bridge, A. J. had her mail forwarded and changed bank accounts. When Rose Marie knocked on her door she acted as if nothing had happened and threw her arms around her sister making a scene in front of her kids saying, "Look who's here, I guess your Aunt decided to come see you after all." Later the kids told their Aunt Rose Marie their mother had told them their Aunt didn't really love them and they had to move so they wouldn't be hurt anymore because she didn't want to see them. After that, Rose Marie was careful about how she treated A. J. knowing she was capable of not letting her have contact with her nieces and nephew

"Do the kids know about Jonathon?"

"Of course, they do, I told them we can't spend any money because their uncle is a lousy rat and they have to get jobs to help pay the bills because I can't work, I have to stay home with the 'little one' especially now that I have an eighteen-year-old. His father doesn't have to pay unless he goes to college and he says he's not going. What am I going to do, sis? I just hate Jonathon for what he did."

Rather than trying to explain things to A.J., Rose Marie assured her things would work out. "Please don't hate Jonathon, we don't know what has happened or why this has happened, A.J. So, let's pray for him that he's alright. I'm sure everything will be fine once we get a chance to talk to him."

*****

Assuming Rose Marie had called her siblings, Annabelle began to read over her notes for the umpteenth time, trying to see something she had not seen before. "Why can't I see it?" she said aloud with both hands on the sides of her face as she slowly pushed back her long black hair. She was convinced there was something in her notes she had missed. Something kept nagging at her but the more she read the less she knew. A woman was in the picture now and she needed to know who and what she had to do with this case. *Was he having an affair with someone back before*

Doris died? Why did Jonathon need so much money? Where did all the money go? It was a large sum, adding everything together it was close to a million dollars not including the house.

Beginning to get a headache, she stood and walked to her kitchen, took out the canister containing her favorite blend of coffee. She poured water into the reservoir. Then adding coffee beans to the grinder, absentmindedly pushing the lever, she ground and ground until the beans had turned to a fine dust. Realizing what she had done she dumped the grounds in the trash and started again. While the coffee brewed, she walked to where she kept her mahogany-front file cabinet. She pulled the Bordeaux file and laid it on top of her desk before heading back to the kitchen where she poured from the pot her favorite pick-me-up. Back at her desk with the cup of fresh brewed, very dark coffee, cupped in her hand she looked down at the file folder.

Hours later, coffee pot dry, headache gone, the only thing that stood out, and then only slightly, was a reference to the death of a husband of a friend who had died of mysterious causes. It was not much, but in the morning, by now only a couple of hours away, she would call Sidney with the information.

"Well, you're right it's not much, but on the other hand it's all we have. Any idea whose friend it was?" Sidney asked.

"That's the sticky part," Annabelle hesitated.

"Lay it on me, I can take it," Sidney said mockingly.

"Rose Marie's."

"Whoa, that's heavy," he paused then, "I guess the first stop is Rose Marie."

"Tread lightly Sidney, we don't want her going out on her own, she could really mess things up if she knew this might lead us to Jonathon. She really cares about him but she's very fragile right now." Annabelle warned.

"Got it, I'll be careful. As a matter of fact, I may not ask her directly, maybe it was in the newspaper. I'll start there."

"Good idea let me know, goodbye."

Chapter **15**

The alarm clock rang loud and clear as Sidney and Leslie lay quietly next to each other, lost in their own thoughts. Leslie hit the off button and laid back down. She took a deep breath then asked Sid? "Why don't we have a few friends over Saturday night I'll get a cake and we can ask our friends to bring their favorite dish."

"Sounds great, hon you want me to do anything?" Sidney said getting up on one elbow and giving Leslie a kiss. She shook her head in answer to his question, then he rolled over to his side of the bed with feet on the floor and headed to the bathroom. She heard the shower water running and then Ryan let out a scream announcing he was ready to begin his day.

Throwing her robe on, she went down the hall to Ryan's room. Reaching the door, she tied the sash around her waist cinching in the green satin material over the matching nightgown hugging her body and hoisted Ryan from his crib.

"Good morning, handsome, let's get you changed and go see your daddy off."

Giving Ryan a kiss, then a big hug for Leslie, he slung his briefcase strap over his shoulder, "Back to the mines sweetheart, have a great day. I'll be spending my day at the morgue and in the news, office going over stacks and stacks of newspaper copy."

"Oh, I wish I could go with you, but Daisy is off today and I'm going to try to work at home, too bad, have fun," she said laughing as he went down the steps of the porch.

"Hey, maybe you could go online and check the Newspaper Archives," Sidney said hopefully.

"If I can work around Superboy, I'll try to do that," she answered.

*****

Sidney looked at the clock on the wall across the room, it was 12:30 and having skipped breakfast, he was starving. Remembering the date of the paper he had just scanned, he stood up and stretched. With briefcase in hand, he headed for the door.

"Hello Sidney, what brings you to The Times-Picayune this morning?"

"Hey Derik, how have you been, we haven't seen you guys in months, kids tying you down. I know our little guy is, we hardly go anywhere anymore."

"That's right a little boy, how old is he now?" Derik said walking along side Sidney as they went out on the sidewalk. "How about some lunch, I'm buying."

"Sure, Ryan is eighteen months now, walking, getting into things and climbing on everything, well you know with four of your own."

"Just wait until he starts playing pee-wee ball, that's when the fun starts, then multiply that by four, and there are not enough hours in a day. Is this okay? They have great seafood here," Derik said as the two men walked and talked then turned into a café.

"Sure, this is fine," Sidney said getting in line with Derik.

After placing their order, they sat down in a booth. The café was not far from the newspaper office, and Derik told him he ate there several times a month, usually with his reporter going over copy for the headline to hit the paper in the morning.

"You can't have the headline this early, what if there is breaking news? Do you leave it to the TV stations?" Sidney asked.

"Oh no, that's a dirty word around the newspaper, we always prepare for last minute changes, the front page is the last to go to press," Derik told him.

"So that's why the ink is still wet when I get my paper," chuckled Sidney.

"Speaking of headlines, what are you working on, anything interesting?"

Saved by the server setting their plates in front of them, Sidney didn't answer but took a big bite of his shrimp taco. "I was starved, these are good," Sidney told Derik who gave him a knowing eye.

"So?"

"You know I can't tell you anything about a case, Derik."

"I know this much, you're friends with the Murphy's and that lawyer, what's her name, Annabelle something or other, local gal, big-name attorney now," he teased.

"Robicheaux, Annabelle Robicheaux," Sidney responded.

"So, what gives, are you working on the Jonathon Bordeaux disappearing act?"

"And if I were, I would spill the beans right here, so you could go stop the presses with a big scoop."

"Well, something like that," Derik grinned.

"No. Can. Do. Mr. Editor. You'll have to find out some other way, but not from me."

"As I suspected, you're chasing leads on this disappearance, I hear they found his boat. Do you suppose he's going to stay in Mexico? He has all but sealed his fate, hasn't he?'

Wiping his mouth with a napkin, Sidney took out his billfold, and laid a few bills on the table and told Derik he was getting the tip. "Thanks for lunch I appreciate it, I need to get going, it was good to see you again."

"Let's get together some time, I mean the four of us socially, no strings attached." Derik teased.

"Yeah, maybe we can do that, but leave your pen and pad at the office," Sidney retorted.

Then getting up, Sidney said good-bye leaving Derik to finish his meal while he headed back to the newspaper office.

A couple of hours passed and still nothing, then turning the page he saw the headline and immediately knew he had struck gold. Jotting down the information he carefully stacked the papers neatly, as not to leave a clue for anyone anxious to see what he found. He left the building feeling excited about the information, knowing finding the name of the woman in the mystery could be the big break in the case. Not wanting to take a chance on revealing his discovery, he pulled to the side of the road and looked up the address on his cell.

The house was in the Mid-City, a typical New Orleans style painted a dark green with wood-stained shutters, was in a well-kept, middle-class neighborhood with front yard, grass, and sidewalks. He pulled to the curb and scanned the area then notepad in hand went up the stairs to the front door and rang the doorbell. When no one came to the door, he knocked loud enough for anyone to hear.

"She ain't home mister," a juvenile voice from the sidewalk said.

"Do you know how long she's been gone?"

"Yep, I been taken care of her yard, mowing, stuff like that," the young boy said with the pride of a business owner.

"So, when is she coming back?"

"Don't rightly know for sure mister, she just told me to take care of the place, and she would send me my pay,"

"And, she has sent you money ever since she's been gone?" Sidney said walking toward the boy.

"Sure enough, just got my pay from her yesterday, she sent it from somewhere in Texas. I guess she's on vacation 'cause the other checks came from right here in Louisiana," the boy said starting to get back on his bike.

"This place in Texas, do you remember the name of the town?"

"Yeah, it was a guy's name," the boy said scratching his head.

"Allen, I think, Yeah, that was it, Allen."

"Could it have been McAllen, Texas?"

"Yeah, it was McAllen, Texas."

"Thank you, you have been very helpful, and by the way you're doing a great job on the lawn, it looks really nice, I'm sure she will be pleased when she gets back," Sidney said patting him on the shoulder.

"Thanks mister, if you need your yard done give me a call," he said with a grin and handed him a hand-made business card, that Sidney stuck in his pocket.

Back in the car, he jotted down some notes and then called Leslie and asked her to invite Annabelle to dinner, so they could talk in private.

"Sure, no problem, have you found out something?"

"Yes, possibly something real important, Les, how are you and Ryan doing?"

"Great, we went to the park and had lunch up on the corner at the cute little place where everyone made over the cutest boy in town," Leslie said. "And before you ask I didn't look at the archives."

"Down girl, take it easy, we know he's the cutest boy in town, but other people have children too, and they may think their little boys are the cutest in town," he said teasing her.

"But they would be wrong, right?"

"You win, he's the most handsome, almost nineteen-month-old around, and don't worry about not getting online, I found what we are looking for, now get on the phone with Annabelle and I'll see you later. Do I need to run by the grocery store and get anything for dinner?"

"No, I think I have everything, see you this evening. I love you."

That evening, after complementing the cook several times, Sidney poured them a glass of wine.

"Okay, spill the beans, did you find her?" Annabelle said pushing her bowl over for another helping of jambalaya.

"Not exactly, but I think I know who she is."

"Betty Jean, Bonnie Jane, like the initials on the boat?" Leslie said.

"Wait a minute, Mrs. Bordeaux's name was Betty Jean. He named his boat after his mother, after all he did, that's unbelievable," Annabelle said leaning back in her chair.

"Well, there are more unbelievable things coming up. Her husband's name was Harold Trudeau, the son of another prominent lawyer," Sidney said winking at Annabelle in acknowledgement of her status in the community.

"You're kidding, how do you know it is the same one?" Leslie said intrigued.

"Well, I talked to this kid and got lots of information, down to the town where they may be staying as of yesterday. McAllen, Texas, which, by the way, is not far from where they found his boat down by Matamoras, Mexico. So, I booked a plane ticket for tomorrow morning," Sidney explained and told them of his discovery at the newspaper, and his conversation with the kid in the lawn mowing business.

"So, what's her name and what did the article say about the death of her husband?"

"It wasn't front page news, it was buried in the second section of the paper, but it did state that there were some questions concerning Harold's' death. I didn't see any other reference from that day forward, it was like it just went away."

"Her name, Sidney," Leslie said anxiously as she stared him down.

"Margaret."

"Of course, Margaret Trudeau, she was on the historical society committee, I think she was the chairman. I remember now, her husband died unexpectedly. Since nothing else was reported, do you suppose her father-in-law tried to make something out of it that wasn't there," Lesley said.

"What a wonderful mind, Lesley, always thinking of new plots of interest for your books," Annabelle said. "I'm interested in how Jonathon and Margaret managed to hook up and what are they running from or maybe who."

"My thoughts exactly, I think I can snoop around in McAllen without fear of being noticed because Jonathon doesn't know me. Wait a minute, how does Rose Marie fit into this, I thought Margaret was her friend," Sidney asked Annabelle.

"If I remember correctly, Rose Marie, her mother Betty Jean, and Margaret were on that committee together, and when Dad drew up the trust, he made a note of a friend of Rose Marie losing her husband in questionable circumstances. My Dad was always good at taking notes and putting them in the files for future reference; he always said you never know where something someone says will lead. He sure was right in this case. Without that note, we may not have found Margaret. So, thank you, brilliant lawyer that you were, Dad, for keeping notes."

The three musketeers, back together solving mysteries, could not contain their abilities to weave clues and characterize the people involved in the case they were working on. They worked well together bouncing ideas off of each other, and this case was not unlike the mystery of Annabelle's husband Dean's death. Jonathon's case was full of unanswered questions, and as each discovery raised its head, more questions came to light. They now had some clues to go on and they began to work on piecing the puzzle together.

"Do you think Rose Marie could shed more light on the subject," Lesley said

"Like I told Sidney, I would rather not talk to her just yet, I'm afraid she may do something foolish to protect her brother, so for now let's keep it just between us."

Chapter **16**

Constant decisions, phones ringing, people popping into his office to ask questions was what he thrived on, and nowadays it kept him from thinking so much about Jonathon. However, he couldn't help but wonder what kind of mess his older brother was in, and he felt guilty, in a way, that he couldn't help him. He and Jonathon had never been real close; he had guessed it was the age difference. Not only did they have opposite personalities, but their likes and dislikes were not even remotely the same. Jonathon was more laid back, easy going, whereas Jeffrey was fast paced, on-the-go, constantly looking for the next challenge.

Although he found it hard to admit, this thing with Jonathon bothered him… bothered him a lot, oh, it was not the money, it was the idea of it that kept Jeffrey awake at night, wondering how someone could do this to his own family. *He had to have a good reason, but what was the reason?* Jeffrey asked himself again and then again. *Did he feel entitled in some way?* Now with his boat found close to Mexico, it was not only certain he was guilty but also, he was not going to face the music. He just never thought of Jonathon as a coward or for that matter an embezzler.

"Hello Katrina Louise, you finally decided to return my call I see," Jeffrey, said kidding with his younger sister. "How are things going in your world?"

"Not bad, sold that house over by the cemetery, made a fat commission, enough to pay a few months' mortgage payments on that house I bought a while back."

"Yeah, how's the renovation going on that place?"

"Really good, I had to find some replacement windows which wasn't fun. I finally found some that came out of another house, they were in a salvage place, and they fit perfectly. Just luck I guess. How are things with you? I guess you heard about our family criminal running off to Mexico. Can you believe that guy? What on earth is the matter with him?" she said exasperated.

"I wish I knew, he sure is dragging down the Bordeaux name, but I guess he didn't think about that when he started stealing from our parents."

"Tell me about it, my clients actually asked if I was related to that 'Bordeaux the embezzler' can you believe it?" Katrina Louise said.

"Dad worked hard to have the things they had, and he was proud of the Bordeaux name. After all, we go back five generations of Bordeaux's right here in New Orleans. Dad would be so hurt and Mom, well it would have killed her had she known," Jeffrey said.

"To be honest, I always thought A. J. would be the one the family would be ashamed to claim, but this situation with Jonathon trumps anything she's done so far, not saying she couldn't do something now, Rose Marie told me she's really desperate now that her son turned eighteen and won't go to college, so no child support for him. She's never worked a day in her life and I don't see her even entertaining the idea of getting a job now. Like a loose cannon, she could explode any minute and no telling what would happen then."

"Probably more headlines to smear the Bordeaux name," Jeffrey said trying to get his head around being bitter on the one hand and having sympathy on the other. He twirled the pen around in his fingers as he absentmindedly listened to his sister ramble on about A. J. and Jonathon.

"Sis, have you been in the house lately?" Jeffrey said interrupting her.

"What? You mean mom and dad's place. No, it's been months since I even drove by let alone go in. I don't know, maybe if we had gone in, we would have seen things missing, but I kind of felt like I would be intruding or trespassing or something, I don't know. How did you feel about the old house, did you go in after the folks died?"

"No, but didn't you think it strange that Jonathon didn't ask your advice on selling the property?" Jeffrey said still twirling the pen.

"I asked him if he wanted to list it and he told me he was going to buy it from the trust at fair market value, so I left it at that. Why?"

"Did you wonder where he would get that kind of money? The house must be worth eight or nine hundred thousand, where would he come up with that kind of money? He and Doris lived a very modest life, I wonder if his house was mortgage free or maybe he cashed in on an insurance policy on Doris, but then why would he steal every red cent from the trust? None of it makes sense, unless…"

"Unless what, what are you thinking?"

"He may have had a gambling problem, which would explain a lot. He could be running from a bookie, you know he could be so far in debt he couldn't pay it back." Jeffrey said sitting up in his chair. "It's the only thing that makes any sense, don't you see he's a gambler plain and simple and we never suspected."

"Well, it certainly would explain where the money went and why he's running, maybe he isn't running from the law but from the people he owes money. Which is worse, being locked up in jail where the outside has inside buddies or being on the lamb trying to stay one step ahead of everyone?" Katrina Louise said.

"If that were the circumstances and it was me, I think I'd be running too."

"The thing that puzzles me is there was never any indication of this behavior before, do you remember anything that might reveal that he had a problem with gambling?" Katrina Louise asked.

"No. I can't think of anything, but nothing else makes any sense." Jeffrey replied still thinking about his brother and wondering if he had missed something.

His conversation with Katrina Louise had shed a different light on his feelings about his brother. His gambling theory had, for the time being, dispelled some of the anger building within him but now there was a reason. He even began to feel sorry for Jonathon and for the first time in a very long time he bowed his head and asked God to keep his brother safe from harm.

Chapter **17**

Piercingly loud clashes of thunder filled the dark night following brilliant streaks of bright lightning flashes dancing across the sky illuminating Leslie's room with intermittent white light. There was a severe storm warning out up and down the coast from Biloxi Mississippi to Brownwood Texas as the first tropical storm of the season churned the ocean waters in the Gulf of Mexico. The sky opened pouring heavy rain pounding against the window panes. She hurried down the hall to Ryan's room at the sound of his screams of fear and taking him into her arms; she held him tight.

"It's alright baby, momma's here, don't cry sweetheart, look its just rain," she said rocking back and forth trying to soothe him. He was holding on so tight that Leslie couldn't pry him away. Then another flash of light followed by a loud clap of thunder made Ryan curl up into Leslie's chest as his little arms surrounded her head.

Leslie began to laugh as she tried to peel Ryan off her, finally free, she sat in the rocker with him on her lap and began to sing

Amazing Grace. About an hour later, the storm moved inland taking the thunder and lightning with it. She laid her little boy back in his bed still humming the hymn and went back to her room just in time to catch the phone before it woke Ryan.

"Hello."

"Hi hon, how's the weather there?"

"Well, I just got your son back to sleep, the thunder was pretty bad for a while. How's it going there?"

"Same, the thunder is pretty strong right now, but it was pouring rain earlier. I rented a car and did some checking in the fancy hotels, figured they wouldn't change their mode of operation but came up blank; then I checked some of the car rental places to see if they had rented a car. For all I know, they bought a house and a car," Sidney said frustrated.

"Don't give up Sid, you'll come upon something, I'm sure."

"I know I just hate being away from you and Ryan, especially in a storm."

"Sid, don't worry about us, we're fine. I've been watching the weather while we were talking, and the storm is actually calming down," she said trying to reassure herself as much as Sidney.

"I love you, Les. I miss you, and I guess I'm just lonely, I used to do this all the time before I met you, but things really change when you find your life partner."

"I love you too, Sid, and that's really sweet, what are you going to do now?" she asked hearing the thunder through her cell phone.

"Hunkered down here at the motel until morning, then if I can't find anything here, I think I'll go toward the gulf and maybe find where Jonathon docked his boat. Anyway, I'll check with you in the morning and be sure to call me if the weather gets bad again, good night honey I love you."

Just then a load noise with the sound of glass breaking broke the silence. Holding her breath to hear more clearly, she walked toward the door. Still holding the cell phone in her hand, she went down the back stairs to the kitchen.

"Leslie, are you alright?" Sidney said.

"Shhh," she said into the phone.

Then she saw the broken glass in the kitchen window over the sink. Easing Sydney's concern, she informed him that a branch had fallen and broken the window.

"I love you, Sid, good night, sleep tight," Lesley said wishing he was beside her, protecting her but she knew better than to share that with him as her imagination was playing tricks on her with the sound of each strange noise. *Heavenly Father, I praise you as you fill my heart with joy and gratitude for your love and protection of my family. Thank you, Lord. Please keep Sidney safe, and Father take away my anxious thoughts as I care for my baby in this big house alone without Sidney here. In Jesus' name, amen.*

Dark clouds still hung overhead when Sidney came out of his motel room the next morning, although the rain had stopped, the threat was still there. And, according to the weather report the chance of rain was more than 80%. He took a deep breath against the high humidity and headed for the rental car.

He threw his bag in the back and put his briefcase in the front seat. Starting the motor, he turned on the air conditioning. Looking at the map he determined the best route out of town toward the gulf. Disappointed he'd not been unable to locate where Jonathon was staying he backed out of the parking space, then pulling forward, he noticed a couple coming out of the motel office. Straining to see, something told him it was Jonathon and Margaret. He watched as they walked in front of the rooms stopping at number 11 then saw Jonathon put the key in the door, open it and follow Margaret in shutting the door behind them. Jonathon was sporting a beard and his hair had grown longer but Sidney was sure it was him. The woman with him fit the description to a tee, except that she was wearing a blonde wig. *Thank you, God,* Sidney prayed.

Not wanting to raise any suspicions, Sidney drove to the end of the parking area and backed into a parking spot. He called Annabelle's office and left a message then prepared to survey the comings and goings from his vantage point where he could scope the whole parking lot. Stomach growling from lack of food and his head beginning to throb from the lack of caffeine he was tempted to go to the café within eyesight to get some breakfast, but knew as sure as he did, he would lose track of them.

Still no sign of them, he sat in the rain that was so heavy at times he could hardly see across the parking lot. Finally, Annabelle called back, and Sidney filled her in. They decided to call the New Orleans police departments, so they could have local officers pick Jonathon up. Just as Sidney was about to hang up from talking to Annabelle, the couple came out of their room and walked to the other end of the parking lot away from where Sidney was parked and got in a car. Turning the ignition, Sidney waited to see which direction they were going. He told Annabelle what was happening and said he would call her back.

The car passed by in front of him as he pretended to read something, then the car turned right, out onto the highway. Sidney waited then followed at a safe distance; they turned into the restaurant not far from the motel. Sidney drove on passed keeping them in sight in his rear-view mirror making sure they were staying put then he backtracked, pulled into the same parking lot a few cars down, and went into the restaurant. Not wanting to attract attention, he sat at the bar where he could see them through the mirror behind the counter.

His cell phone rang, and he saw it was Annabelle, pushing the answer button he said, "Hello."

"Did you follow them?"

"Yep"

"Are you still with them?"

"Sweetheart please stop calling me every five minutes. I'm not going to leave you behind; I just got hungry, I'm right down the road at this place called 'Big John's.' I'll be back in about thirty minutes. Okay?"

"Okay, I'll tell the police, they will either pick them up at the restaurant or the motel."

"You can't walk down here in the rain. I'll order something for you and bring it back, and don't you think that would be better?"

"Okay, tell the police to pick them up at the motel, but Sidney in case they don't go back to the motel, I'll have them keep an eye on the restaurant, too.

"Okay baby, see you soon," Sidney said putting the cell phone back in his pocket.

The couple's breakfast came about the same time as Sidney's. He saw two plain clothes police officers come in and sit at the counter next to him. They struck up a conversation and he told them about having to take a breakfast back to the motel confirming they were in the right place, as he was sure Annabelle relayed their conversation to police as a way of identifying Sidney.

"Can you believe she wanted to walk down here in the rain? I know it's not that far from the motel back there but she just wants to check up on me. Women, sometimes they just don't make sense."

They all laughed and then Sidney got up left a tip and took the takeout sack with him. After paying his bill, he turned back to the officers sitting at the counter and told them to have a blessed day, then he went to his car and waited. Soon he saw one of the officers at the counter leave and get in his car close to the driveway entering the parking lot.

The detective sitting at the counter noticed what appeared to be an intense conversation at the booth where the couple sat. He observed the waitress pouring them more coffee then leaving their bill. Then the blonde woman abruptly got up and went to the back toward the restrooms. The man stayed in the booth as if waiting for the woman to come back.

Sidney noticed a dark-haired woman coming out a side door of the restaurant and heading toward the car he had seen early with the couple inside.

"Wait a minute, that's Margaret, but where is Jonathon?" he said aloud. Too late to signal the police he decided to follow her. As she pulled out of the parking lot, he pulled in behind her. A break in the traffic gave her the opportunity to pull out onto the highway leaving Sidney to wait his turn in the rain now coming down in sheets under dark clouds causing the streetlights to come on. Finally, getting another break in traffic, Sidney maneuvered out of the parking lot onto the highway, now covered in puddles of water making driving even more difficult, but he still had her taillights in view, as she was having to slow way down to avoid hydroplaning. Suddenly a flash of lightning hit a tree in front of his car and a large branch came crashing down onto the road in front of him causing him to slam on his brakes as the car slid sideways coming to a stop before hitting the barrier as he helplessly watched her taillights fade into the rain-filled horizon. Backing up, he managed to turn around and head back to the restaurant, arriving in time to see the detectives leaving. They stopped alongside his car, and he rolled down the window.

"We lost them, they just disappeared, where did you go in such a hurry?"

"I followed the woman but she got away when a tree branch fell in the road in front of me, but where is Jonathon?" Sidney yelled above the noise of the rain.

"He went to the restroom and gave us the slip. We found the woman's wig, big bag and coat in the lady's restroom, but no sign of Jonathon."

"Maybe they will meet back at the motel," Sidney said.

The detectives took off toward the motel and once again, Sidney tried to turn around. Something caught the corner of his eye at the back of the building, and there in the pouring down rain was Jonathon crouched on the ground by the dumpster. Sidney stopped the car got out and walked toward the back of the building, as soon as Jonathon saw him he jumped up and ran with Sidney fast on his tail. Jonathon tripped over the curb and Sidney tackled him.

"Jonathon, we're too old for this cop and robber thing, come on man, it's over, are you hurt? You took a pretty good spill." Sidney said feeling sorry for him. As he looked into his face, Jonathon looked old and defeated, something no man wanted to be at any level.

"No, I'm okay, who are you?" he said brushing his wet hair out of his face.

"Sidney Rye, I work with Annabelle, I'm a PI."

"Thank goodness I thought you were a bounty hunter." Then without warning, he started to laugh at his thought process, *here you are soaking wet thinking you're being taken down by a bounty hunter and all along, it was a PI working for Annabelle.* Sidney joined him in laughter as he helped him up and they went to the car and got in.

"You've had your sister worried, she really cares for you. Rose Marie and Patrick are good friends of ours."

"Sidney, can you just take me home?"

"I have to turn you into the authorities, Jonathon."

"But, could you take me into your custody? Couldn't Annabelle vouch for you to the authorities?"

'I guess she could, if she were willing, but you have a new charge against you Jonathon, it wasn't smart of you to disappear. Why did you run?"

"It's a long, complicated story that I'm not ready to divulge just yet."

"Okay let me call Annabelle," Sidney said taking out his cell phone.

After his conversation with Annabelle, he called Lesley.

"Les put a candle in the window, I'm headed home and I'm bringing Jonathon with me."

"That's great, we have missed you, and how is Jonathon?"

"Okay," then turning to Jonathon "do you want her to call Rose Marie?" he said.

"No, she'll know soon enough," Jonathon said in a low voice.

"She really should know, how about I let Annabelle tell her?" Lesley told Sidney hearing what Jonathon had said.

"That sounds good. I'll be home after dinner so go ahead and eat something."

"No, I'll wait for you, I love you," Lesley said.

Annabelle guaranteed the safe return of Jonathon with the DA's office, calling off the detectives in Texas. So, Sidney stopped at the motel went in with Jonathon, and they both changed out of wet clothes into dry clothes from their suitcases. It was obvious a woman had also been in the motel room, but Sidney ignores that fact for the time being. Back in the rental car, they drove to the airport, checked in the car, and purchased tickets back to New Orleans. Jonathon was glad they wouldn't spend hours together on the road thus avoiding in-depth conversation. Finding their seats, they settled in for the short flight.

"We'll be back home soon," Sidney said putting his carry-on in the overhead compartment.

"Back home," Jonathon said, "will I ever be back home?"

"Well, Jonathon, the police will meet us at the airport, sorry man. I can't take you any further than the airport."

"Thanks, Sidney, I appreciate your kindness," Jonathon said. "I know you must be full of questions, and I really appreciate you not pressing me for answers. I just realized how different my life would be going forward. There's a good book I read one time about the fact you really can't go back home. I guess that didn't cross my mind when I started making decisions that would undoubtedly change my world forever. I know things don't stay the same and change is inevitable, but my decisions have led me to a change I never bargained for and as naïve as that is, I never thought I'd end up on my way to jail for the second time, of all things."

"Life can surely present some challenging choices but no matter where those choices lead you, Jesus will be there walking beside you. Even in your darkest hour, Jonathon, you can depend on Him being there for you. I know this for a fact, I have seen a lot in this business and I have made a few mistakes myself but with the help of my Savior, Jesus Christ, I have come through it as a better person. So, turn things over to Jesus and the road ahead will be easier, sure you'll have to face the consequences of your actions but with Him by your side you can face them with your head held high. Ask forgiveness of those you have hurt and relieve the burden of guilt you carry," Sidney said with a conviction Jonathon could not ignore. "Jonathon, I do need to tell you, if the woman you were with had anything to do with this whole mess you should tell the authorities, or she may be gone forever leaving you to hold the bag."

Jonathon lowered his head and made no comment.

Chapter **18**

Sidney's words filled his head the rest of the flight back to New Orleans. Being handcuffed again and taken off by the police to the looming jail seemed unreal. He had enjoyed freedom briefly after skipping bail but now knew it would probably be a long wait to experience freedom again, if ever. Back in the cell, he began to look at the situation from a different perspective.

Looking over the past few years of his life, he could not help but wonder what put him on a path that led him to jail. His marriage to Doris was happy enough, though mundane to the point of routine. He would get up in the morning, eat the breakfast she prepared, then walk a few blocks on the sidewalk down Pirate's Alley to his Clock Repair business. He sat on the same stool for twenty years, at the same table surrounded by tools of his trade, repairing neglected clocks; then he would break to eat the lunch she prepared. At the end of the workday, he would walk back on the same sidewalk to the modest two-bedroom Creole cottage he and Doris shared and have their dinner in silence. After cleaning up and washing dishes, they would watch TV while she crocheted. They had no pets, no friends to speak of except for a few neighbors they spoke to on occasion when they found themselves outside their homes at the exact same time. They didn't go to plays, concerts, movies or even out to eat. They didn't own a car, so they either walked or called a taxi to go shopping for groceries. Sometimes he would stop at a neighborhood store and get milk or bread on his way home from work. They never sat in the shared courtyard full of tropical plants behind their cottage. They lived in the colorful French Quarter and yet never experienced the atmosphere around them.

"What a dull existence," he thought to himself, "no wonder Margaret was able to entice me into her schemes, she represented excitement, adventure… even to the point of abnormal… something I never had with Doris."

Jonathon met Doris at the library during his college years where he studied nearly every evening and would see her sitting at the next table. Not bad to look at she seemed shy, not unfriendly just quiet and he would smile at her when he would catch her looking at him. After a few weeks he got up enough nerve to actually sit across from her at the table where she always sat. She reminded him of a puppy he once had that was the runt of the litter, not mischievous like the others but content to sit on the sidelines and just watch. It took many evenings in the library before she agreed to go out with him.

"Doris would you like to go get some ice cream at Brahms's?" he would say.

"No thank you, not tonight," she would answer.

Then one night he asked her to a movie, and she accepted only to tell him later she didn't eat ice cream because it made her sick.

Several months went by before he popped the question. "Doris would you be my wife?" he said, and looking oh so shy, she answered "yes."

They eloped because she didn't have any family to invite or take part in a wedding. Raised by elderly parents who had her late in life, he soon realized how unworldly his new bride was, and it was a few weeks before he could convince her to meet his parents.

He loved Doris and was content with their life, as dull as it seemed now, at the time he had become used to it and over the years it seemed normal. He became acquainted with Margaret through his mother who had recommended her son when Margaret needed a good clock repairperson for an antique clock belonging to her grandfather.

As Jonathon struggled with the care of Doris, as she lay dying of cancer, Margaret would come to their home several times a week offering to help, bringing food, staying with Doris while Jonathon went to his shop to check on the building. During Doris's illness, Jonathon's business was failing due to his continued absence. Margaret offered to loan Jonathon money, which he hesitated to take but eventually was left with no choice. He appreciated the help Margaret gave him and his wife and was always grateful. Jonathon suggested he ask his family for help and Margaret would tell him not to disturb his family that she could help him and was very willing to do so.

After Doris's funeral, Margaret helped Jonathon get rid of Doris's clothes, jewelry, and medical equipment including medication. They started spending more time with each other as Margaret took care of Jonathon financially while he tried to rebuild his business. Then the phone rang one day, and when Jonathon answered, Margaret's voice, almost inaudible told him her husband was dead. Jonathon consoled her and said he would be right there, but she told him not to come because people could misconstrue their relationship, especially her father-in-law.

He was beside himself as days went by and no word from her. He read the notice in the paper about her husband's death and for the first time realized her husband was the son of a prominent New Orleans lawyer, Shelby Trudeau. At the time the sentence in the article that indicated her husband died of mysterious circumstances, never registered with him.

Several weeks had passed, and then Margaret contacted him, and he found himself talking about how lonely he was and how hard it was to fill his time.

"We were in a routine, I knew what to expect from one minute to the next, and now I just feel lost. Nothing to do, no place to go, I just sit and stare at the walls," he told her.

Margaret seemed to understand, as a widow herself, she began to console him when he would hit a rough spot in the grieving process. Sharing her own struggles with losing a spouse seemed to help him deal with his new life as a single man.

Their relationship was slow in maturing but once started it grew very fast, almost too fast for Jonathon. They went to a restaurant on the lake early in their relationship and watched the sailboats. Margaret told him she had always wanted to own a sailboat. She asked him if he would want to go sailing in his own sailboat. He told her the thought had crossed his mind since even as a boy he loved watching sailboats. She said that he really needed some excitement in his life and after all, he had the money coming from the Estate. So, they went looking at sailboats. He enjoyed her enthusiasm and before he knew it she had convinced him to purchase a very large sailboat with money he didn't have, thus the beginning of a long line of mistakes.

Now in the solitude of his cell, his reveries were filled with unpleasant thoughts of his activities, grabbing him over and over again. When rain pounded on the roof of the building he went to a place of sheer fear remembering how Margaret convinced him to take the sailboat, and with her, escape to Mexico. He was not an experienced sailor, and the thought of open water navigation brought rapid heartbeats and beads of sweat to his brow.

At the dock where the sailboat was moored they prepared for the trip with Jonathon taking on supplies the day before. After unsuccessfully trying to unwind the rope from the cleat, Margaret took a knife from the toolbox and cut the rope releasing the boat from the dock, then he maneuvered out of the slip, hitting the side of the slip a couple of times before headed west. She told him if he was so afraid to go out into the gulf then he should stay close to shore, but not too close, in case the authorities were on their trail. At first, he felt he was in control of the vessel however as time went on he was faced with humongous waves slapping at the sails tearing them from their ties. After struggling to secure the sails, he went back to the boat's wheel. Relying only on the motor, he pushed on, hoping the weather would hold, as increasingly blackening clouds threatened to catch up with them.

He could feel the wind and water as he forced his way through the waves lapping at the bow, lifting the front of the boat, causing a pounding as it hit one wave after another. Barely able to keep the rudders going in the right direction he held on to the wooden spokes as if his life depended on it. His stomach churned with each roll of the waves when finally, on the horizon he could see land and hoped he was able to bring the boat to a docking place. Coming closer to the shore, a line of posts guided him to a safe place to dock and pulling in port side he yelled to Margaret to engage the hawser. Her blank stare told him his boat knowledge was foreign to her, so he pointed to the rope and yelled for her to tie it to the cleat or hook on the post. For a brief moment, he thought she was going to go overboard and it scared him to think that would solve all his problems, however she managed to keep her balance as the waves persisted, raising the boat up then down.

Just the thought of every scenario during that experience put him in a prayer of thanksgiving. He often wondered why God chose to save him, and for what was he saving him. Lessons learned, maybe, or was God's plan bigger than that? Was he saved just to spend the rest of his life in prison? These many thoughts haunted him as he tried to come up with reasons for his own actions and God's saving grace.

Chapter **19**

"Hello," Annabelle answered the phone then putting her pen down she leaned back in her office chair waiting for the voice on the other end.

"Annabelle, its Jeffrey, do you have a minute?"

"Sure, what's up?"

"I was wondering if you know anything about what's going to happen to Jonathon now that he's back in jail."

She could hear the concern in his voice and wanted to reassure him, however she wasn't sure what she could do to help Jonathon at this point, so she kept the conversation factual avoiding anything that would give him false hope. At the same time, she tried to keep her own feelings in check as just the sound of his voice brought back the feelings she had that night several weeks ago when they had dinner.

"Thank you, Annabelle, I really appreciate your candor, by the way I know it has been a while since we went to dinner, but I'd really like to have dinner with you again sometime if you'd be available," he said hoping for the best.

"As a matter of fact, I'm starving. if now is a good time, I'm available," she said.

"That's great, I'll pick you up in… say an hour," he said.

Annabelle took a deep breath and went to the bathroom to freshen up. Looking in the mirror she once again felt conflicting feelings, one of guilt, and one of desire. Guilt because of her happy marriage to Dean and now she was having a desire for another man. She reminded herself of the loneliness, the longing for a man's touch, someone to go to the theater with, have intimate dinners with and laugh at private jokes with. *Dear Father, I'm so grateful that you're in my life. Thank you for watching over me. I ask that you give me peace and understanding about this situation with Jeffrey. In His name, I pray.*

Brushing her thick long black hair, she pulled it up into a bun secured with bobby pins, then put black liner on her eyelids and bright red lipstick on her lips and finished with a touch of blush on her round cheeks. One last look satisfied her desire to look her best then she went back to her office just in time to see Jeffrey come through the office door.

"Wow," he said noting her French creole beauty. "I'm sorry I just didn't remember how beautiful you are, now I'm blushing."

"Thank you, you have made my day, and flattering will get you absolutely nowhere," she said laughing aloud then grabbing her purse and gloves she walked through the door he held open for her and watched as he pulled it shut checking to see if it locked behind them.

Out on the street, he took her to his car. She tried not to think of the gesture similarities between Dean and Jeffrey. He held the car door for her and then went to the driver's side just as Dean had always done. It was so comfortable to be with Jeffrey even with the mixed feelings surrounding her.

"I decided to drive instead of calling a taxi, so we could go to a place I know about in the Garden District to eat. Is this alright with you?" he asked in front of the Commander's Palace.

"Oh yes, I love this place," she said.

There was silence during the examination of the menu, then Jeffrey asked her what appealed to her? After her selection of Barbequed Gulf Shrimp, he agreed and placed an order for two of her choice, then winking at Annabelle, told the waiter to bring two citrus coolers.

The conversation during dinner was accelerating as one subject after another presented itself, and each started a completely new adventure in knowledge, commencing with the daily news, business finance, political ideas or finally religion.

"I have always admired Rose Marie and Patrick. They searched until they found the faith that fit their beliefs, unlike me. I regret that I have not been entirely true to myself where faith was concerned. How about you?"

"Well, I, like you, was raised a Catholic as many here in the French Quarter were. However, I left the church when I was in college. Then when I married, my husband was a Catholic, but we were both looking for something we didn't find in the Catholic religion, and we joined a small group of believers who study the bible. After Dean died I found it hard to go back among friends we made together. But, with Joe and Sadie Sully's encouragement, I rejoined the study group and I'm finding it refreshing to learn from the Bible teachings again. It's really been a blessing to me.

I'm closer to God than I've ever been. He's in my life daily, in everything I do, and I can't tell you how much that means to me. I used to be afraid of a lot of things, but now with God in my life, I just turn it over to Him and trust His will in all things. That doesn't mean I'm foolish, like I don't run around on the streets by myself in the middle of the night just to test Him, but when things happen that are scary, I trust in His promise."

"Wow, I could use some of that kind of faith."

"Would you like to come with me this Sunday? If you don't want to go to the Rye's, where Rose Marie and Patrick go, we could go to the Sully's. I think they are having a meeting at their place on Sunday."

"You know what, I think I'm going to take you up on that and it probably would be easier if Rose Marie and Patrick were not there. Thank you. Thank you for the invitation."

*****

Annabelle could not wait to get home and call Leslie. The phone rang and rang and then the voice mail. Annabelle left a message hoping Leslie would return her call right away, and then she remembered to call Leslie's cell phone.

"Hello"

"Leslie, you're not going to believe what I'm about to tell you," Annabelle said sharing every detail of the evening even the part about her making sure she looked ravishing when Jeffrey came to get her.

"Oh Annabelle, that's wonderful, how exciting and great idea about going to the Sully's. They will show him how down to earth they are and how simple to just believe and trust in the Lord. I'm so happy for you Annabelle. Hold on a minute Sidney wants to know what's going on."

Leslie turned to Sidney and shared the news, then back to Annabelle she said, "Great things happen when we turn it over to God, Sidney and I can tell you that," she said winking at Sidney.

"Well, we have only had two dates, but yes, it is working out. Leslie, it is so good to be with a man again. We had so much to talk about, on every subject in the world it was just wonderful, and he's such a gentleman…. I want to say like Dean, but I cannot be comparing the two of them."

"You're right, this is a new beginning for you, yes Dean was the love of your life, and you'll always love him no matter what, but let Jeffrey into your life. He can fill the void that was left by Dean, but he will never replace him," Leslie told her.

Chapter **20**

Staring at the ceiling of his cell, he let his mind wander and as usual, his thoughts went back to the beginning of his relationship with Margaret and he wondered where she was and if he would ever see her again. Sitting up he put his feet on the floor and got off his cot, looking around he felt the four walls closing in on him and began to pace around the eight-foot square trying to relieve his anxiety that overcame him as he heard moans, groans, screaming and yelling from the other prisoners. *How did I get myself involved in embezzlement of all things, I'm not a criminal? Why did I let this happen? Was I so vulnerable that I let myself be manipulated,* he thought. Then he remembered what Sidney told him on the plane. *Whatever happens I'll depend on God to walk with me.*

Later that day he was told someone wanted to see him, and the guard took him to a room with a table and two chairs. Not knowing what was coming next, he bowed his head and began to pray, *Father I ask you to be with me in whatever is about to take place.* Looking up from his prayer, there standing in front of him was a young clean-shaven man in a dark suit.

"Hello, my name is Mitchell Irving, I'm the public defender assigned to your case," he said offering his hand to Jonathon for a handshake.

"I don't want a public defender," Jonathon loudly proclaimed refusing his handshake.

Mitchell dropped his briefcase on the table and sat down. "Well, since you have no assets and you skipped bail, letting you out on bail again is out of the question, and you can't afford an attorney, so why don't you tell me what led to you embezzling your parents' trust fund," Mitchell said tapping his pen on the table.

"Let's say I did this but there were circumstances that forced me to do it, how would you defend that?" Jonathon asked.

"You mean circumstances forced you to buy a boat, fancy car, max out the credit cards and mortgage your parents' home?" Mitchell said still tapping the pen creating a drumming effect in the background.

"Well, it's obvious you've already decided I'm guilty as charged, so how can you possibly defend me with that kind of attitude? Is it because you couldn't come up with money to start your own practice, so you took this salaried job with the courts or let me guess you have lots of money and you're doing this out of the kindness of your hard heart. Well, Mister Public Defender I don't need you or want you representing me." Jonathon said getting up from his chair. Noticing the pen tapping had stopped he said, "I would get a grip on your lack of patience, that nervous habit of yours is a distraction and how do you expect to hear someone explain anything with you tapping that pen the whole time someone is talking? Guard!" Jonathon called and walked through the door never looking back.

*****

The next day he again was taken to the room, but this time it was the attorney he had hoped would represent him.

"Hello Jonathon, how are you doing?" Annabelle said sitting across the table from him.

"I'm okay considering everything. How are you and my brother Jeffrey doing? And please don't deny it I saw you at the restaurant the night I got out on bail," Jonathon said with anger in his voice.

"Jonathon, we were both hungry, and your brother was worried about you and wanted some answers, so we went to dinner to talk about what might happen if you were found guilty. Now since that night, we have had dinner together again, and Jeffrey plans to attend a meeting with me this Sunday. Does that answer your question?" Annabelle said as calm as she could.

"Yes, it occurred to me after seeing you two at the restaurant that you and Jeffrey had a thing going and that's why you wouldn't represent me. They assigned a public defender to me yesterday and he's a real jerk. I fired him before we even got started. You're the only one that I feel safe with telling my story to, Annabelle. "

"Who is the public defender?"

"Mitchell Irving."

"He's a good PD. I've known him a long time and he'll do a good job."

"I don't want a public defender, I need a good lawyer and your reputation precedes you, Annabelle. I'm in serious trouble, more serious than you know, and I could be facing a life sentence without your help, so please hear me out."

Chapter **21**

Leslie flipped her laptop open and began proofing, while taking a sip of the coffee the waiter brought to her, as she waited for Sidney. Excitement filled her head as she thought about finishing this book. Staying in the cottage was a good move. It allowed her uninterrupted work, and she was able to complete the book in half the time if she had stayed home to write.

"Hi sweetheart," Sidney said leaning down and giving her a squeeze. "How has your day been?"

"Really good, it won't be long until this book is on the shelves."

"Great then we can start on the studio," Sidney said.

"Wait a minute, mister. You just got a big assignment from Annabelle, and I have a great idea for another book, so when do you see us having time for this big project."

They ordered lunch and changed the subject for the time being. "Jonathon must be a good salesman to get Annabelle to take his case," Leslie said.

"I know, I was surprised when she called, and I didn't even ask how the family felt about it. I can see that some of them are indeed going to be upset. I just hope Annabelle knows what she's doing. Again, how's she going to be paid?" Sidney rhetorically asked Lesley.

"Well, let's just hope she knows what she's doing, but I do have faith in her ability to give Jonathon a fair and honest defense," Leslie said putting her laptop away as the waiter set a bowl of sausage gumbo in front of her.

"Boy, this smells so good," he said blowing on his spoon, "and it tastes as good as it smells. It's almost as good as Joe Sully's, speaking of which I hope that goes well with Jeffrey and Annabelle this Sunday at the meeting. That was a great idea she had, inviting him to go with her."

Lesley agreed and wondered if Rose Marie knew he was going with Annabelle to the Sunday meeting. Sidney told her she would certainly be happy about it if she did know. Then finishing their bowls of gumbo, they walked out into the sunshine. They said goodbye with a kiss and went their separate ways.

That afternoon, Lesley sent the final file to the publisher and called Annabelle. She didn't answer her cell, so Lesley called her office.

"Robicheaux," Annabelle said.

"Hi, just wanted you to know the book is ready for press," Lesley said with a sigh of relief.

"Oh, Lesley, that's great.... I'm actually going to miss you sitting back there with those fingers flying over that keyboard. What are you going to do now?"

"I have an idea for another book. However, Sidney and I had lunch today, and he wants to start on the studio. So, you know I would have to be there, but I had a thought. How about I help you two with the research?"

"Say, that's not a bad idea. Do you think Sidney would be all right with it?"

"I can certainly talk to him about it and let you know. It'll be like old times," Lesley said excited to get started.

*****

"So, what do you think? Annabelle thinks it is a great idea and I could do most of it from home," Lesley said enthusiastically.

"Okay, you have talked me into it, I think the first thing you could do is a background check on Margaret and her husband. There is something about all of this that does not compute. If you get my drift," Sidney said. "I'll check with Annabelle and see which direction she wants to go."

"Great then I can get started tonight after Ryan is in bed."

"Wait just a minute, young lady, that's our time, you can start in the morning," he said giving her a kiss on the cheek.

Leslie was making progress on the background check of Margaret's husband, Harold Trudeau but was finding it harder to find much on Margaret Trudeau. They were only married for three years, and the wedding certificate filed at the courthouse listed Margaret as Margaret Anderson of St. Louis, Missouri. On further investigation, nothing came up under that name around Margaret's age or residence. So, Lesley started running down the Margaret Andersons listed that didn't fit the profile.

Margaret P Anderson was from Chicago Illinois and 39 years old, married with two kids. Margaret J was from California, single and 23. Margaret A listed with several relatives and lived in Louisiana. Lesley put a bookmark on that listing and continued down the list. Margaret M was living in Longview TX, 61, no known relatives. Another possibility she thought as she kept scrolling down finally finishing with three strong possibilities. The last suspect was a Margaret Louise last known address Wichita, Kansas, 58 with two deceased husbands listed.

Then, on a hunch, she began to check initials, M Anderson, M A Anderson, and so on until she ran across an M Anderson in New Orleans with one relative listed, a Jason Anderson. A son maybe, she thought, staring at the screen. Could she have a son living right here in New Orleans? She looked up the names, and since Anderson was such a common name, there were many listed. However, one stood out. Jason Anderson was 47, lived in New Orleans, and as Leslie checked his background, she discovered he had a criminal record. She wrote down the last known address and called Sidney.

"Good work, sweetheart, I'll check it out."

"Be careful Sid. He could be dangerous."

"I think I'll just put surveillance on for now and see where that leads us. I sure would like to know if Margaret is in Mexico," Sidney said. "If this is her kid, he may lead us to her, in which case that would be a real break."

"I'm going to see what I can find out about this guy's mother, so far the records are pretty sketchy, but maybe something will show up," Leslie said.

Sidney had not told Leslie everything Annabelle had shared with him, and for now he thought it best if she didn't know. It would just worry her and the research she was doing would keep her occupied as long as she didn't run across anything revealing about Margaret.

He needed more information about Margaret, and perhaps Jonathon could fill in some blanks, so after putting Charles Bordet, his trusted agent, on surveillance, he decided to pay a visit to Jonathon.

At first, Jonathon was surprised to see Sidney, then he remembered that he worked with Annabelle. Shaking Sidney's hand, the men sat down.

"How's it going, Jonathon?" Sidney asked.

"It's not fun, but I must say that little mini-sermon you gave me on the plane has truly helped. I never got a chance to thank you for that. I honestly appreciate everything you did to make a difficult time easier for me, thank you, Sidney."

"You're welcome glad I could help. Now the reason I'm here. Annabelle told me you're aware that we are trying to track down Margaret and I was hoping you could help us fill some holes. Do you know if she had any children?"

Jonathon thought for a minute then shaking his head he said, "Not that I remember her saying. She did talk on the phone to someone now and then, but she said it was her nephew."

"Can you remember any names?"

"Let's see, it seems like she called him Josh or was it John, oh Sidney I can't remember for sure," he said trying to recall the name.

"Could it have been Jason?" Sidney said thinking about the information Leslie found.

"Could have been, that sounds right, I know it began with a J like my name because I commented at the time about how her nephew's and my name both started with a J."

"Did she ever make any calls from your cell phone?"

"Maybe, but they put my stuff in lockup somewhere, maybe the DA has it. Can you find out? Will you be able to get it if it is important?"

"I'm pretty sure that can be arranged. Can you remember anything else that might be important... names, places; did Margaret talk about her family other than her nephew?"

Jonathon sat staring at Sidney as if he was a stranger, his mind whirling in his head as he tried to recall something, anything that would help Sidney. Then almost under his breath, he said, "She did talk to Doris a lot and one day she didn't know I was standing behind her in the hall as she talked. She told Doris her last husband Benjamin had gone fast, didn't know what hit him and she was sure Doris wouldn't feel any pain either. At the time, I thought she was trying to make it easier for Doris. She also told me after Harold died that her father-in-law had made sure Harold didn't have her in the trust for at least ten years after their marriage. She was very upset about that and told me she was glad he died when he did so she didn't have to honor that trust by staying married to him for ten years."

Sidney assured Jonathon they were working hard on his case and reminded him again that God was with him. Back in his car, Sidney called Leslie with the information he thought could help, then headed for the DA's office to retrieve the cell phone.

Chapter **22**

When Annabelle announced that she was taking Jonathon's case, the siblings were stunned. Rose Marie took it as a sign that Jonathon was innocent. She knew Annabelle wouldn't have taken his case if she thought he was guilty. Jeffrey was surprised but didn't approach Annabelle about it. The siblings realized that she could not represent them as they had been asking her too, now that she was representing Jonathon. Each one had their own opinion, and some shared openly.

"How can she defend Jonathon when she knows he took our money?" A.J. said after Rose Marie told her the latest news.

"Have you ever considered the fact that he may be innocent?"

"Innocent? Are you serious? Didn't he run from the law? If he were innocent, he wouldn't have run."

Not wanting to get into an argument that would only fuel A. J.'s fragile state, she didn't pursue the conversation, instead asked her if she and the kids wanted to come for Easter Dinner.

"Katrina Louise and Jeffrey are coming, and Patrick is smoking a turkey," Rose Marie said hoping she could convince her to come and bring her kids. A.J. said she would think about it and let Rose Marie know.

"Is she coming?" Patrick asked.

"She's going to think about it. She's angry that Annabelle is taking Jonathon's case, and I must admit I'm wondering why Annabelle changed her mind. Don't get me wrong I'm so glad she's representing him, but don't you want to know why?"

"She obviously believes his story and since we don't know what his story is we have to trust Annabelle's take on this and allow her to do her best for Jonathon. Sidney is working on the case. So, who knows, Leslie may be involved in this also. I understand the three of them do work well together." Patrick told Rose Marie.

"I pray every day this will have a good ending and Jonathon will be out of jail. I'm not kidding myself. I know it didn't help his case any when he skipped out on his bail. Oh, I wish I knew what was going on with him and why he did this."

"I know honey, let's just trust God with this and keep praying for Jonathon. Let's remember P*hilippians 4:5. Be anxious for nothing, but in everything by prayer and supplication, with thanksgiving, let your requests be made known to God.* It's in His hands."

Chapter **23**

"**D**o you think it could be time for us to talk to Rose Marie about Margaret?" Leslie asked Annabelle as the three of them were having lunch.

"She may be able to add some information to the mix, like did she know Margaret's husband and does she know if Jason is her son," Sidney said.

Annabelle sucked in her lower lip, as was her habit when she was not sure how to answer a direct question. Staring at her, they waited for her answer. Slowly letting her lip take its normal shape again, she shook her head. "I'm not sure that would help us at this point. I think I would be more interested in what Margaret's ex-father-in-law has to say about her. Leslie, I hear he's kind of a lady's man, would you be comfortable interviewing him?"

Leslie looked at Sidney before answering. "What do you think?" she asked.

"I think it might work, as long as he doesn't put the move on you, I'm okay with it, if you want to do it."

Sidney had made business cards with Leslie's maiden name in anticipation of just such an occasion. So, after studying some background information on Trudeau, Leslie prepared for the interview.

*****

"Hello, my name is Leslie LaRue. I have an appointment with Mr. Trudeau," Leslie told the receptionist.

"Yes, Ms. LaRue; he's expecting you."

"Come on in here, Ms. LaRue. What can I do for you?"

"Did your secretary tell you I'm with Rye Private Investigators?" Leslie said handing him her business card across the desk as she sat down in the large leather chair that swallowed her small body.

"I see, well what's this about?" he said a little irritated at the thought she was working for this Rye character. He had run into him several times during trials where he was a witness for the other side.

"I understand your deceased son Harold was married to a Margaret Anderson."

"Yes, this is true. Why do you ask?" he said intrigued.

"We are working on a case that may involve your former daughter-in-law, and we would appreciate any information you may have about her," Leslie said noticing the look on his face at the mention of his daughter-in-law.

"What kind of case are you working on, if I may ask?" he said sitting back in his chair, trying to look curious but unconcerned.

"It could be a criminal case. She's missing. Would you have any idea where she may be?" Leslie said avoiding any pertinent information.

"A criminal case you say, very interesting. I must confess, I've always had my doubts about her. I even ran a background check on her when she married my son. However, I didn't find much, except that she had another husband, or maybe two husbands before my son married her. When my son died, she had him cremated before I could get an autopsy. I did insist my son have a clause in his trust keeping her from any monetary reward until after ten years of marriage, however I think she milked him dry with her charm. She was a conniver, if you know what I mean. I never trusted her. Harold even put their house in her name, bought her a fancy expensive car and a plethora of designer clothes and jewelry."

"Did you ever hear mention of her children?"

"No, I was never aware that she had any children of her own. My son mentioned the only family she had was a nephew or was it an uncle. I honestly don't recall for sure."

"I'm sorry to bring up old memories, but it would be helpful if you could remember anything that would shed some light on who she is or was and where she is now," Leslie said standing up.

"I wish I could give you more information and maybe after I have thought about it a while I could remember something that would help. I didn't like her and wondered if she had anything to do with my son's death. He died so suddenly leaving a big void in my life. I guess I have tried to put it behind me and go on, but the fact that she may be involved in something criminal would sure answer some of my questions," he said with a look of sadness on his face. "My son Harold was a good man but a little naïve especially when it came to women."

Molly Owen

"Thank you, Mr. Trudeau. We will be in touch with you if we learn anything, and we would appreciate any information you may remember," Leslie said allowing him to shake her hand that he seemed to hold a little too long before releasing.

As she reached the door, he remarked, seemingly having gotten over his sadness, that perhaps if he remembered anything they could talk about it over drinks.

She repeated her thank you and continued through the door into the reception area where she stopped long enough to speak to the receptionist. *It never hurts to be friendly to the screener,* she thought. Using her given name gave her an edge she probably wouldn't have otherwise. *Sidney was so smart to put her maiden name on her cards.*

*****

After dinner, they stood side by side at the kitchen counter washing and drying the dishes. Putting the plates in the cabinet, Sidney realized that neither one had said anything since they cleared the table. He wondered if Leslie was as deep in thought as he was about her conversation with Trudeau. Finally folding the dish towel and leaning back against the counter he cleared his throat.

"Did you say something?" Leslie said

"No."

"I've been thinking," Leslie said tapping her fingers on the handle of the faucet.

"Not again. When you start thinking, it is either a new plot idea for a book, a change to the plans for the studio, or a conversation you had with someone. Hopefully, it is the conversation you had with Trudeau. Am I right?"

"Well, you must admit he was a little vague. I think he knows more than he's willing to tell us. Do you think Margaret had something to hold over his son's head? Or, even more intriguing, is she holding something over Jonathon's head and that's why he did all of those things? I just can't imagine Jonathon being that naive, can you?" Leslie said staring at the wall across from them.

"Oh, I love it when your wheels start to turn. It's like watching someone putting a jigsaw puzzle together."

"Think about it Sid. Rose Marie keeps saying this is not like Jonathon. So, why would he do those things?"

"Good question. The explanation Jonathon gave to Annabelle is not the whole story. Annabelle and I both knew that when she told me what he said. So, you're probably right. Why would Margaret be so fast to cremate her husband's body unless she was trying to hide something?"

"And what happened to her other husband or husbands?"

"I wonder if she has some connections in Mexico or if she just went there to get away from Jonathon. I better have another talk with Jonathon. I think it is time we asked some important questions about his knowledge of Margaret's life before he came into the picture, now that he has had time to mull things over."

"Good idea and I'll continue to research Margaret's past."

Chapter **24**

Jeffrey found it hard to concentrate as of late. He had not asked Annabelle about the murder of her husband hoping she would bring it up. He knew she was a skilled attorney and wondered how she managed to convince the police that her husband, Dean, didn't commit suicide, as reported in the newspaper but was, in fact, murdered. This ability of hers was exactly what Jonathon needed in a lawyer, someone to believe in him enough to find out what actually happened.

One afternoon, Jeffrey looked on his cell phone and saw a text message from Annabelle. She was in court, and could not talk, but wanted him to meet her in about an hour on the square in front of the St. Louis Cathedral. He sent a message back that he would be there. He was concerned because she rarely sent him a text but this one sounded urgent.

She was sitting on the concrete ledge that held the black iron fence around the square. Texting on her cell phone, she didn't see him walk up. Standing before her, Jeffrey waited until she finished texting then said hello as he sat down beside her.

"I just wanted you to know this before you heard it from some other source," she said putting her cell in her pocket.

"What is it?" He said anxiously.

"Someone at the newspaper got wind of an investigation we are working on, and it's all over the front page," she said

"You mean about Jonathon?"

"Yes, but it is more than that, we've been searching for a woman he was involved with hoping we could find out more before it was made public" she explained.

"A woman? Who was she?"

"That's just it Jeffrey, Rose Marie and your mother served on a committee with her and probably introduced her to Jonathon. Her name is Margaret, and she was married to the late Harold Trudeau, son of the prominent attorney Shelby Trudeau."

"Do you mean Jonathon was having an affair with this Margaret?"

"We are not positive about their relationship but are convinced they were in this together. Now before jumping to conclusions, let me just say that I believe, and so do Sidney and Leslie, that she was the ringleader. We have been searching for her, and we think she may be in Mexico."

"Sidney and Leslie know about this?"

"Yes, they are working for me and running the investigation into who Margaret is and what she's doing in Mexico. Now, please do not jump to any conclusions about anything especially what you read in the newspaper. Leslie and Sidney have gone over to see Rose Marie hopefully before she and Patrick see it in the paper."

"But, who would have leaked this information to the newspaper?"

"We have some ideas, but I cannot share them with you, you understand."

"Sure, I know you and the Rye's are on top of this."

"Keep us in your prayers, Jeffrey, this is getting dangerous."

"Dangerous? How? Are you in danger?"

"Probably not, but Sidney and Leslie could be because of the things they have uncovered."

Jeffrey sat stunned thinking about Jonathon being involved with something that could put people in danger. What on earth has Jonathon gotten himself into? Who is this Margaret person? What does my mom and sister think about her and why did they introduce her to my brother?

"I better go see Rose Marie right away. She will be devastated if she thinks she had anything to do with this mess," Jeffrey told Annabelle as they stood up. "Are you sure you'll be alright?"

"Yes, go on, I'm going back to my office and Jeffrey I'm sorry. I know this is hard to understand, but we will get this back on track."

"I know you will," he said.

Back at her office, she called Sidney to see if there was any action at Margaret's son's place where Charles was doing surveillance.

"So, do you think he will contact his mother when he reads the paper?" Annabelle asked.

"Surely that's what he'll do if in fact he's her son and knows her whereabouts," Sidney said. "And by the way, Leslie is hot on the trail of the previous husbands. She found out that they too were cremated soon after their death. With no autopsies in these deaths, who knows why they died. It also appears that the marriages were short-lived, and the men's previous wives had died also."

"Could it be that she's a serial killer since she's leaving a familiar trail?" Annabelle said out loud as her analytic mind stirred the facts together.

"It sure sounds like it. And I would like to keep a tighter rein on Leslie's involvement in this." Sidney said with concern.

"I agree but remember; she doesn't listen to advise very much when it involves danger. Perhaps we can keep her busy with research and keep her out of the field." Annabelle answered.

*****

After Sidney's conversation with Annabelle, he decided to run by the office before going home. Instead of using the parking lot at the side of the building he left the car parked on the street. He sensed something was wrong as he approached the door to the building. He saw a flash of light at the back of the office.

Stepping back, he called the police telling them to keep the sirens silent. He took his gun from the holster and putting himself in the shadow of the building waited for the police. Just then he felt a blow to the back of his head as he stumbled but managed to keep his balance. A figure ran ahead of him, then ran to the parking lot, and soon a dark sedan pulled out and took off down the street. Sidney put a call into the police and gave them a description of the car. Feeling faint, he sat down on the sidewalk and waited for help.

"You alright?" the officer said.

"Not sure, I have a dilly of a headache and kind of sick to my stomach."

"Well, we lost your friend and came back to see if you could shed some more light on this apparent break-in. But I think we need to get you to the hospital. Anyone you want us to call?"

"He may have gotten my gun," Sidney said shaking his head.

"Is this it?" the officer said holding a pistol up.

"Yes, that's it."

"We thought it might have been dropped by the runaway," He said with a chuckle then helped Sidney to his feet and put him in the patrol car.

"I'm okay, it's just a precaution. I'll call you from the hospital as soon as I'm checked out," Sidney told Leslie over the cell phone. "Yes, call Annabelle, it could be the suspect in the case we are working on," Sidney said cautiously. "And call Charles and have him check the office and see if anything is missing."

*****

"I'm so thankful that you're alright Sidney," Annabelle said sitting across from him at the dining room table while Leslie went to see about Ryan.

"I'm fine. We just need to stay on top of this before someone really gets hurt," Sidney said getting up.

"Just a minute, Mister Rye, you're not going anywhere. A concussion and six stitches gets you a break from cops and robbers for a few days," Annabelle scolded. "Leslie and I can keep up the research and Charles can do the legwork. You just rest and get back to normal."

"Whatever normal is," Leslie laughed as she entered with Ryan in tow. "I wouldn't know normal if it hit me in the face. Ever since I met you two, I have found myself in the middle of danger."

"And you love it," Annabelle smiled at her.

"Well, I use to," Leslie told her. "Until it hit real close to home. I don't like it that someone knew where to find Sid and maybe he knows where to find us."

"Don't worry, sweetheart, we're safe here."

"Margaret's no dummy, Jonathon probably told her about us and where we live. Now she will tell her son and who knows, she herself may even come back to take care of business. I don't like it, Sid."

"I know Les, but we'll just have to be careful," Sidney reassures her. "I remember a time when you would dive right into danger without a thought for your safety."

"Yes, I remember those times," Annabelle agreed.

"That was when I was foolish and unaware of the change in one's outlook when one becomes a mother," Leslie said giving Ryan a squeeze. "So, we'll just have to be smart about this investigation and not take any chances. Agreed?"

After Annabelle left, Leslie put Ryan to bed kissing him on the top of his head and laying him down she thanked God for her little boy. As she shut the door to his room, her mind began to play tricks on her. It was always difficult to keep from being concerned about Sidney's line of work, and the danger he was often in but to add to that concern, her child and his safety was nearly unbearable.

Sidney was aware that Leslie was dealing with anxiety over Jonathon's case and wanted to ease her mind as much as possible. However, he was also concerned especially after tonight. This case was taking a more serious turn that could involve murder. *What is Margaret up to? Will she come back like Leslie believed? How involved is her son?* These questions were swirling around in his already hurting head when Leslie came into their bedroom and without a word went to the bathroom and shut the door. He could hear her crying, and he went to the closed door.

"Les, can I come in," he said almost in a whisper.

"Yes."

Putting his arms around her, he let her cry. He knew words wouldn't fix the situation, so he just held her until she could compose herself. Soon she raised her head from his chest and with one more sniffle said, "I love you, Sid."

He pulled her close to him and said, "I love you too, Les. It'll be alright."

Lying next to each other in bed, both in their own thoughts, Leslie took Sidney's hand. "I'm glad you're okay. I don't know what I would do without you."

Sid squeezed her hand then drifted to sleep, filled with uneasy dreams of unpleasant situations.

Chapter **25**

Rose Marie could not believe the things she was reading. Even though Sidney and Leslie tried to soften the blow, it was even harder to see it in print. The words seemed to jump off the page and hang in the air like a thick fog. How was this possible? She read it again and then out of frustration crushed the newspaper in her hands and threw it down on the floor in front of her.

Patrick was sitting quietly as she read, waiting for her reaction, and now he watched silently as Rose Marie stood up with a look on her face that Patrick didn't recognize. Without a word, she went to the kitchen and began filling the coffee pot with water. Taking the coffee can down from the cabinet she slowly scooped the grounds into the filter. She just stood looking at the pot still holding the scoop in her hand. Automatically, she pushed the button that turned on the pot. She watched as the water began to drip through the filter.

Her thoughts were racing as she tried to put the puzzle together. Margaret Trudeau? What is her connection to all of this? She's not even in Jonathon's league. What do they have in common? Why wasn't I told about Margaret before this? I can't believe that I was the one who introduced her to Jonathon to have her antique clock fixed. Were they having an affair while Doris was dying? No. that's not something Jonathon would or could do, that just can't be the case. Oh, Jonathon, why didn't you come to me?

She bowed her head in prayer. *Dear Lord, help me with my anger, give me the strength to face whatever is to come. I trust in You, Lord. Be with Jonathon and Annabelle as she sorts through this. In His name. Amen.*

She carried two cups of coffee on a tray to the other room where Patrick waited. Setting the tray on the table, she stepped back and sat down across from him. Neither said a word.

"We have a lot of work to do, Patrick," Rose Marie finally spoke.

Before he could answer, the doorbell rang. Patrick let Jeffrey in and followed him to the living room to join Rose Marie.

"Have you seen the paper?" Jeffrey said.

She nodded in response still trying to control her anger.

"When did you know about this?"

"Just a little while ago," he answered. "I wanted to make sure you were okay."

"Did you know I introduced Margaret to Jonathon?"

"How did you know Margaret?" Jeffrey said avoiding her question.

"Mother and I were on the same committee with her, and she needed an antique clock repaired, and I sent her to Jonathon," Rose Marie said in a matter of fact way, still holding her feelings.

"Did you and Patrick ever see her and her husband socially?"

"No. We did not. We didn't run in the same circles with them. We never had an occasion to socialize with them, and neither did Jonathon. I never met her husband," she said sternly. "Did Annabelle call you? Did she tell you anything we don't know?"

"Yes, I talked to her, but she didn't tell me any more than what is in the paper. She said Sidney and Leslie are both working with her also, but they wouldn't be able to shed light on anything yet."

"Well, Sidney warned us, but you're right he shed no light on the subject," Rose Marie said trying to control her disappointment in her friend. "I guess our brother is the only one that knows the answer to all our questions."

"We knew Sidney was working with Annabelle," Patrick said. "I understand they have all three worked together before. I think Joe Sully told me the three of them solved the mystery behind Annabelle's husband's death."

"I'm glad about one thing. I'm glad Annabelle is Jonathon's attorney. If anyone can get him out of this mess it'll be her," Jeffrey said.

Chapter **26**

The Newspaper article had the Bordeaux siblings in turmoil as each one, in their own way, processed this new information. Robert and Sandy immediately headed back to New Orleans to meet with Annabelle with the hope of finding out the nature of Margaret's relationship with Jonathon.

"Who is this Margaret character, and where did she come from?" Sandy blurted. Before Annabelle could explain, Sandy continued with a barrage of questions. "Were they mobsters or partners in crime? I know, they were lovers and took the money to move to Mexico," she said looking at Robert.

"BE QUIET!" Robert shouted at his wife. "Can't you see Annabelle doesn't have the answers to your insane questions?"

"But………….."

"Close your mouth and listen."

"Sandy, Robert is right I don't have all the answers yet, but as soon as I do, I'll let you know as much as I can without hurting Jonathon's case." Annabelle assured her.

"I honestly don't care about helping him win his case. For that matter, I hope he rots in jail." Robert said turning red in the face and almost gasping for air.

"Please Robert, calm yourself, there's nothing we can do right now, and I suggest you go back home and wait until I've something to tell you," Annabelle said concerned about Robert's face color.

Suddenly, Robert fell to the ground. Annabelle jumped up from her chair and knelt down beside the still body on the floor of her office.

"Sandy, call 911, he isn't breathing,"

Her hands shaking, Sandy reached for her cell phone, her fingers barely able to push the numbers. When the operator came online, she handed the phone to Annabelle. She looked down at Robert not knowing how to feel. *Is he going to die? Now what is going to happen? No money. No husband.*

Annabelle sat with Sandy and Rose Marie in the hospital waiting room anxiously wondering if Robert would live. Patrick brought coffee back from the cafeteria and set it on the table between Sandy and Rose Marie. Annabelle took her cup, and Patrick asked if there was any news.

"Not yet," Rose Marie said.

Another hour went by before a doctor and Chaplin appeared in the waiting room. Rose Marie braced herself for the news to come.

Annabelle gave Rose Marie a hug before she left the family to deal with details, offering to help call the others.

"Yes, that would help," Robert's sister said with a strong voice.

After the arrangements were made with the hospital on which funeral home to take the body, Rose Marie and Patrick left with Sandy in their car and headed back home.

"I'm alright, just take me back to his… my car," Sandy said.

"We'll get your car later. Right now, you're in shock and need to be with family," Patrick said.

Sandy sat stoic, in the backseat, not a tear in sight. She thought about all the times she wanted to leave Robert and how she was afraid he would leave her before he got the money from the estate. Now he was gone and so was the money. She began to laugh hysterically. All these years waiting, living a loveless marriage and now this was the way it ended. She knew Robert had everything in his name, so she would be penniless, not a dime to her name. That was his plan all along, she thought.

Rose Marie looked at Patrick then turned to look back at Sandy. "Are you alright? Do we need to stop the car?" But Sandy kept on laughing until eventually, the tears came, not of sorrow for her husband's death, but for her own future.

Patrick stopped the car and Rose Marie got in the backseat with Sandy. She put her arms around her. "Sandy, we love you and we're here for you. You're part of this family and we, with God's help, will see you through this, I promise"

*****

"Jeffrey, I have some bad news," then as gently as possible she broke the news. "I'm at home, do you want to come over?" she said.

"Yes, do you mind?"

"No, not at all. Would you call Katrina since you two are close and I'll call A.J.?" Annabelle said.

The pain in Jeffrey's voice resounded in her ears as she put her cell phone down. Two blows in a matter of days would take a toll on anyone, and she knew Jeffrey's strength was waning. At the Sunday morning prayer meeting, just two days ago, Joe talked about trusting in God's promise to be with us in our time of need, and she remembered telling Jeffrey how Jonathon had begun to read the bible and how he would ask her and Sidney questions when they went to see him. This seemed to lift Jeffrey's spirit, but now she wondered if he would be able to trust the Lord as much as he should. Rose Marie and Patrick's Christian foundation would see them through, but the brothers were just now learning the wonders of God's blessings. Annabelle bowed her head in prayer. *Father, thank you for your Grace Lord for your hope for your children I praise you. I ask that you be with Jeffrey and Jonathon on the loss of their brother. Lord, please bring them peace. In Jesus' name, Amen.*

Her long conversation with A.J. was full of questions she was unable to answer, either from not knowing the answer or the answer would have jeopardized Jonathon's case. A.J.'s concern for the death of her brother was minimal. She and Robert were not close, and she let Annabelle know she could not stand his wife, Sandy. She wanted to talk about the newspaper article and if they could bring suit against 'this Margaret person'.

"She's the one with all of our money and she should be made to give it back," A.J. told Annabelle in a loud voice causing her to remove the receiver from her ear. As expected, A.J. was not at all satisfied by Annabelle's replies. The conversation ended with A.J. hanging up without saying goodbye.

Annabelle took a deep breath trying to clear her head before Jeffrey arrived. She found herself anxious to see him. He had never been in her home and she hurriedly cleared her desk of papers putting them in files and returning them to the file drawer in her desk. Satisfied with the rest of the room she decided to make a pot of coffee to go with some sweet rolls she picked up from the bakery. Little did she know, after Dean died, she would be entertaining a man in her home? Her nervousness was coming to the surface and she jumped when her cell phone rang.

"Oh, hi Leslie... Yes, it happened in my office. I'm waiting for Jeffrey to come over and Leslie, I'm nervous."

"Why on earth are you nervous?" Lesley said.

"I don't know. I guess because I'm really falling for him," she said hoping Lesley would understand and give her some pointers.

"Annabelle, be yourself. He's hurting and wants to be with you," Lesley said gently. "Just be there for him. Listen, let him share his feelings."

"I guess that's what concerns me. What if he shares his feelings about me?" Annabelle spoke her concerns out load.

"You'll be fine"

When she opened the door, Jeffrey managed a smile and thanked her for letting him come. He wanted to take her in his arms but thought better of it, instead he took her hand and followed her to the kitchen. The aroma of fresh brewed coffee beckoned. He sat at the small table at the end of the kitchen and waited while she poured a cup and sat it in front of him. Taking her cup from the counter, she sat across the table.

Jeffrey had so much to say, even after rehearsing in the taxi on the way over, he was still not sure where to begin. He relaxed when Annabelle broke the silence.

"I'm so sorry you have so much to deal with right now."

Not sure how to answer, he remained silent. Lowering his head, he choked back tears. *What's going on, Robert and I were not close. Why am I getting emotional? This is not how I want Annabelle to see me,* he thought feeling very vulnerable. Taking a sip of coffee, he controlled his need to cry.

"I got these sweet rolls at the bakery yesterday morning, but they are still fresh. Would you like me to heat yours and maybe put some butter on while they are still warm?" she said realizing he was having a hard time with his emotions.

The fact that he was taking the death of his brother so hard was a surprise, since she knew their relationship was estranged. Jeffrey had told her about Robert and how he treated Sandy through the years. In frustration, he told her his feelings for Robert were strained because he didn't think of him like a brother, not even a friend. He said if he had a choice he wouldn't choose Robert as a brother or a friend. This realization bothered Jeffrey because it involved family.

Annabelle took his nod as a yes and began to warm the roll. With her back to him, he felt he could say something without breaking down.

"There are or were three brothers in my family and even though we were never close, I always wished we were more like brothers like the ones I saw in other families. Developments over the past few months have brought these many issues I've dealt with over the years to the surface. When I think about my relationship with God during those times, I'm brought face to face with my shortcomings and I realize I should've made a better effort with both my brothers instead of basically cutting them out of my life as if they didn't exist. Going to the Sully's for prayer meeting renewed my relationship with God, but I'm sure you're wondering why I'm reacting this way. It's because I'm sorry I didn't try harder with both my brothers and now one is gone forever and the other is in serious trouble."

Annabelle put the sweet roll on the table and turned to Jeffrey. Without a word she put her arms around his shoulder and gave him a hug. Then leaning back, she told him.

"Jeffrey, we all have regrets after losing someone. That doesn't make us a bad person. The fact that you're concerned indicates you're a kind, compassionate, loving person. I see that in you. God sees your concerns and your heart," Annabelle said sitting down across from him.

"Thank you, being around you has helped," he said with a chuckle.

"I don't know about that. I think you came to me that way."

"Boy, do I have you fooled," he said giving her a wink.

They finished their coffee and sweet rolls and went to the living room where they were much more relaxed. Their conversation went to Rose Marie, knowing how this would affect her. Her family seemed to be coming apart at the seams. As they talked, Jeffrey kept staring at the harp. Annabelle had told Jeffrey once that she had not played the harp much since her husband died and now sitting across from the piano with the harp next to it he asked her.

"Annabelle, will you play the harp for me?"

"Now?"

"Yes now. I'll make a deal with you. If you play the harp, I'll play the piano."

"I didn't know you played the piano. Do you have any other secrets you care to share?" She said walking to the harp and sitting on the stool before tilting the instrument back. With expertise, her fingers pulled at the strings then as smooth as silk she rolled her hands across the strings making beautiful music.

Jeffrey, mesmerized by her skillful command of the harp, rose and went to the piano. His fingers found the melody she was playing and in unison they performed a duet.

Tears came to Annabelle's eyes as she remembered how she and her father would play together by the hour. Soon they ended their concert and Annabelle shared her thoughts with Jeffrey.

"You're an excellent musician Jeffrey. Where did you learn to play?"

"Oh, I took lessons for many years as I'm sure you did. I have a piano in my condo that I play often. It's my go-to when I need to relax."

"Well, we make beautiful music together," Annabelle said then realized the implementation.

"Yes, we do," Jeffrey said giving her a wink and a smile. "Let's make sure we do it again."

As they stood, Jeffrey took Annabelle's hand and pulled her to him. Leaning down, he kissed her softly for the first time.

"I've wanted to do that for a while now," he said.

"I'm glad you did," she said. Then regretfully she pulled back from him. "Jeffrey, I need to tell you something before our relationship goes any further."

Puzzled at her actions Jeffrey said, "What's wrong?"

"If people know or even suspect you and I are in a relationship it could jeopardize Jonathon's case." She told him gently.

"What do you mean?"

"The prosecutor could claim it is a conflict of interest and take me off the case as Jonathon's attorney."

"I see, so what does that mean for us?" Jeffrey said feeling rejected.

"It means we cannot give anyone cause for suspicion. This is really serious, Jeffrey, if I'm going to be able to clear Jonathon."

The grief of the day had begun to settle as Jeffrey thanked God for Annabelle, and now she was telling him they would have to put this relationship on hold, for who knew how long, in order for Annabelle to defend his brother.

"That's going to be hard beyond words because I'm in love with you."

"Oh Jeffrey, I love you too. But we must, for Jonathon's sake, not let this become known," she said staring into his eyes. "Jonathon has already misjudged our dinner together, and others could do the same."

Chapter **27**

Sidney felt a responsibility for Jonathon's spiritual health and volunteered to go to the jail to break the news about Robert's untimely death, so he could be there for him as he digested the information. With a prayer for guidance, Sidney left the car and went into the building where Jonathon was being detained until the hearing.

"I didn't know Robert had heart disease. That's awfully young for a heart attack isn't it?" he pleaded with Sidney for answers. "I mean, I know he had a temper and was always unhappy. Did you know they wanted children at one point, but it didn't happen? I suspected Robert was sterile from some things he said, but he always blamed Sandy. I can't believe he's gone. He probably hated me for what I did, and I don't blame him. Sidney, do you think my being in jail had anything to do with his heart attack?"

"Don't go there Jonathan, I understand heart disease starts long before the actual heart attack, so this was going to happen no matter what and you can't take any blame for this," he assured him.

"I can't tell you how ashamed I am for all the grief I've brought to my family. Will they ever forgive me?" Jonathon said. "I don't even know if God can forgive me."

"Jonathon do you remember how Peter betrayed Jesus? How he denied knowing him?"

"Yes."

"Peter moved on from his shame to the forgiveness through Jesus Christ his Savior. God will forgive you Jonathon and in time so will your family. Don't focus on your sins, rather focus on your relationship with Jesus. No matter the future, let Jesus be your guide, let the Holy Spirit lead you."

"God the father, the Son and the Holy Spirit."

"Yes, that's right Jonathon let's say a prayer together."

As they bowed to pray Jonathon took the lead. *"Almighty Father, we praise you and thank you, I thank you for Sidney and his wisdom, God, and you know our grief. I ask you, Lord, to stand by me and my family in our hour of need. I don't know Robert's relationship with you, Jesus, my prayer is he knew you and will have eternal life. You know my shame, I pray you release me from this controlling emotion that I may live in union with you. I love you, Lord. In Jesus' name, I pray. Amen."*

"Amen," Sidney said

*****

Because of all the publicity about their family, already it was decided that the funeral services would be private and unannounced. Still concerned about the safety factor, Leslie felt better about attending the services knowing it had not been in the paper. It was a simple memorial in the chapel at the funeral home with the burial following. Sidney and Leslie said their good byes shortly after the service and didn't stay for the burial because Sidney wanted to be with Jonathon who was not allowed to attend his brother's memorial.

After taking Leslie home, Sidney drove toward the jail while his thoughts went to Jonathon, about how far he had come in his walk with God and how this would go a long way toward his ability to face the future no matter what the outcome of his trial. From Annabelle's information on the case, this could be a trial that went beyond embezzlement because she believed that Jonathon had damaging information concerning Margaret that would have to come out. Meanwhile, Sidney's immediate assignment was to locate the fugitive believed to be hiding in Mexico.

Chapter **28**

The streets of Matamoros, Mexico were extremely crowded. Vendors selling their wares from trinkets to raw meat lined the roads and pathways. Smells filled the nostrils, not like the aromas in New Orleans, the odors that permeated the air were a mixture of sweet and rot. Flies swarmed around the food causing stomach acids to churn. The crowds were a perfect place to lose one's self, but it would have been a lot easier if her fair skin had not been so obvious. Getting through the check-in gate was frightening but she had a fake passport in the name of Maria Garcia. Many cars were crossing the border from Texas, but the patrols were checking for contraband and because she was walking across they didn't detain her more than necessary. Getting rid of the rental car before crossing the border put her on foot. She headed in search of a place to stay. More interested in a private setting rather than a hotel she picked up a local paper. Her Spanish was very good and searching the ads she found one that fit the bill perfectly. Not far from the Market, she asked directions and started walking with purse and shoulder bag in tow toward the room for rent.

Winding through the dirt covered alleyways, she found the one-story house with a picnic table in front under a homemade shelter. The ground was crawling with creatures including scorpions. A short brown-skinned man looked out from under a car and waited for her to speak. In Spanish, she asked about the room for rent. He directed her to the house where she talked to a short little round woman with her hair pushed back in a bandana, rented the room and asked about food availability and the location of the nearest Bank. She had gathered quite a large sum of money and purchased traveler's checks that she wanted in a bank for protection. Once accomplished, she would settle into a new life for herself and her son filled with luxury.

It had been a stroke of luck to ditch Jonathon at the restaurant. She told him she thought that one of the men at the counter was a bounty hunter and that they needed to split up. She told him to walk back to the motel, and she would pick him up there. Poor Jonathon, he never knew what hit him. It was so easy, almost too easy, with Jonathon. He didn't have a clue this was not her first rodeo. After all, he was just one in a long list of suitors she had bilked out of their money including her dumb husband, Harold, even if his father thought he was in charge.

Sitting on the side of the bed in the small room, she made sure the door was locked then took out the traveler's checks and stacking them up in piles she added them up to a total of $750,000.00. Stuffing the checks into a secret compartment in her skirt, she put the skirt and blouse on that she had made for this occasion and headed for the bank. Walking the streets toward the bank, she acted like a local with her hair back in a bun and her colorful long full skirt swishing in the gentle breeze surrounding her not wanting to attract attention like the one she would if she appeared to be a tourist. She got rid of her cell phone while still in the states and was not planning on getting another one until she was settled into her new home. Excitement filled her head as she reminded herself to be very careful. *Now is not the time for mistakes,* she told herself as she entered the bank lobby.

The money safe in a deposit box, she tucked the key in her secret pocket and headed to the nearest public phone.

"Hi, it's me everything is a go," she said in Spanish to the person on the other end of the line.

Silent as she listened. "Find out, NOW, and don't make any mistakes," she demanded. Slamming the phone into its receiver, she stood outside with her mind churning. *What did that idiot do?* She thought. *This is not the time for mistakes. If he can't fix this, then I'll go back and fix it myself.*

Chapter **29**

L eslie, still anxious over Sidney's attack at his office, just wanted to conclude this investigation as soon as possible. She had a theory and was hot on the trail of any clue to tie things together. She wished Annabelle could share more of her knowledge of the case. But she understood the confidential reasons for not divulging too much information.

So, she started at the beginning dissecting the case. She now knew that Margaret was involved with Jonathon before Doris died. *Was there an affair? Or were they just friends? Maybe Rose Marie could shed light on this.* She reached for the phone.

"Hello."

"Hi Rose Marie, how are you doing?"

"A little better than when you and Sidney were here."

"I'm so sorry about Robert. The service was very nice. Joe did a good job."

"Thank you. Yes, he did do a good job."

"How's Sandy doing?"

"Okay I guess, their marriage wasn't good for a long time. I don't know if that messes up the grieving process. One minute she's crying, the next minute she's laughing. She insisted on returning home, I just wish she would've stayed here with us a little longer, I don't think she's very stable right now. But enough about that. How are you?"

"I must say I'm staying busy these days working on Jonathon's case. That's why I called. I know this is a touchy subject with you but could you search your memory and tell me if there was any indication that Jonathon was having an affair with Margaret or were they just friends as far as you know."

There was silence, then Rose Marie said. "Leslie, I have stayed awake at night racking my brain trying to figure out what happened. I liked Margaret, we were not close friends, but through the committee we were on, we seemed to get along just fine. As women usually do, we talked about family and our own lives, and I remember her comment that she had never had children. Her previous marriage was childless, and she stated that this marriage would be barren also. We all gave condolences since we were mothers and grandmothers. One day she mentioned having the need of a clock repairman for her father's antique clock. I told her about Jonathon. Later Margaret thanked me for suggesting Jonathon and what a wonderful job he had done on the antique clock.

"Did you ever see Margaret with Jonathon?"

"Yes, after Doris got sick. One day I took a taxi and went with a covered dish over to Jonathon's. When Jonathon came to the door he seemed flustered, but I assumed it was because he was tired. I followed him into the bedroom where Margaret was sitting with Doris. I thought she was there about the clock. When she saw me, she took the covered dish and left the room saying she would put it in the refrigerator. I heard the front door shut and figured she had left. Doris was unresponsive, just lying there. Her breathing was labored, and her eyes were closed. I asked Jonathon about Margaret being there and I remember he said she would come by on occasion to bring food and stay with Doris while he went to the store. At the time, I thought that was very kind of her, and honestly felt guilty because *I* wasn't doing more to help Jonathon."

"How did you find out that Doris was sick?"

"I ran into Jonathon at the drugstore. He was filling a prescription for Doris. When I asked him if everything was alright he told me she had stage 4 ovarian cancer. I was shocked that we had not heard, but then Jonathon had not been very close to any of us since our folks died. I wish he had told us what was happening in his life. I blame myself for not making more of an effort to renew our relationship. I gave up inviting him and Doris to family dinners at the holidays. I sent birthday and Christmas cards, but that was the extent of my efforts. They were just not social. I think it was Doris. She was very shy and didn't make friends easily."

"Do you by any chance remember what medication Jonathon was getting for Doris?"

"Let me see. Yes, it was a painkiller, a strong one. Not morphine, but something like that. Jonathon said she was in a lot of pain. And Leslie, that night after I saw Margaret at their house, Doris died."

"What about the services for Doris?"

"It was very private, just family and a few of Jonathon customers."

"Did you see Margaret there?"

"No. I didn't see her there and she wasn't at the committee meeting the next month because her husband died." After a long silence, Rose Marie asked what Leslie was thinking.

"Nothing, I'm just putting the puzzle together. You have been very helpful, and if you think of anything else, please call me. We are working hard on this Rose Marie, and we *will* get to the bottom of it. I promise," Leslie said now more confident in that statement.

This revelation about Margaret and Jonathon fit the scenario in Leslie's theory. Not ready to reveal anything just yet, she set out to dig a little deeper perhaps it was time to pay Mr. Trudeau another visit.

*****

"Hello, Miss LaRue. How is the detective business? Here, have a seat," he said putting on his best smile and turning on the charm. "That was quite the newsflash in the paper. Get all the facts right?"

"Not quite. There were a few things left out," Leslie said firmly. "You mentioned the last time I was here that you did a background check on Margaret."

"Yes, I did. Why, did I miss something?"

"I was wondering if you missed it, or was it deliberately ignored?"

"What are you suggesting Miss LaRue?"

"I was checking into your son's background and came across some interesting things. I'm sure you're aware of the trouble he kept getting into, and the arrests that you managed to get him out of many times," Leslie said looking him square in the eye. "It appears his record goes all the way back to his college days. Is that correct?"

Trudeau didn't answer but it was obvious he was not happy with Leslie's findings. "I don't know what you think you've found Mrs. Rye, but I assure you, you're going down the wrong path. Yes, I know you're the wife of Sidney Rye. I too have done my homework. Whatever you think you've figured out, forget it."

"Why? Is that a threat? It seems to me you would want the death of your son exonerated." Leslie said obviously hitting a nerve. "There was an article in the newspaper after your son's death that indicated there was foul play. Do you remember that? And yet it was never mentioned again. Could it be that Margaret had something to do with the fact nothing came of that investigation into the cause of your son's death?"

Rising from his chair he walked around to where she sat and with his large body leaned over her and said, "Miss LaRue or Mrs. Rye whatever you want to call yourself, this meeting is over." Then he walked to the door.

Leslie got up and deliberately walked to where he was standing, then looked up at him. "Think hard about this Mr. Trudeau, this may be your only chance to set things right," she said before walking through the open door that he shut behind her with a slam.

Holding her head high, she walked through the outer office noting that no one was sitting at the desk. Hastening her step, she heard the door behind her open. Turning she saw Trudeau start toward her. As she prepared to run the receptionist came back to her desk and sat down.

"May I help you Mr. Trudeau?" she said.

"No. Not now, Mrs. Rye was just leaving."

Chapter **30**

Feeling comfortable in the fact that Leslie was not about to jeopardize the safety of her family, he was surprised when she told him what she had done. He listened intently to every word wondering where these crazy ideas of hers came from. On one hand, he was very proud of her for following her intuition, but his heart told him the path she was on was a dangerous one if her theory was correct.

"Don't you see Sid, it just makes sense. Why else would he try to cover it up, and why did Margaret lie about having children?" Leslie said pleading with him to understand.

"Even if you're right, Les. This doesn't alter the fact that you put yourself in danger. Why didn't you check with me first? You're so impulsive. You just wear me out when you get like this. I should've never let you work on this case. It's just too dangerous. What if something happened to you? Do you want me to raise Ryan alone without a mother? You saw what happened to me."

"Exactly, that's why *I am* involved. I want this case solved, so we can be out of danger, and get back to our lives. I don't want to raise Ryan alone either," she said tears covering her cheeks.

"Then you do what you do best, RESEARCH, and I'll do the investigating. Understood Leslie?" Sidney said almost ashamed of his demand.

"Sidney Rye. Don't push me into a corner. I know you're concerned but we're in this together like it or not. So, let's stop this right here, right now, and figure this thing out as a team," she said with a firmness that got Sidney's attention.

Without a word, Sidney took Leslie by the shoulders and pulled her close to him. Then he took a deep breath and said, "You're right, forgive me, Les. The thought of losing you is unbearable. I love you more than you'll ever know, and Les I'm very proud of you. I just worry that your need to follow through on your theories into dangerous territory, is going to get you killed one of these days." Then, letting go of her, he quietly said, "I'll call Annabelle."

*****

"She did what? But why would she do that? That's a silly question. We both know she will plunge right in if she's on the trail of discovery."

"We need to talk Annabelle. If Leslie's theory is right, and I'm inclined to think it is, we are all in danger.

"Maybe I should call Jeffrey. What do you think?"

"We could use a stabilizer. Maybe that isn't a bad idea." Sidney said then turning to Leslie he asked what she thought of the idea. She agreed, and Annabelle said she would have him meet her there.

"In the meantime, keep close tabs on our amateur detective," Annabelle told Sidney.

Annabelle called Jeffrey. He was surprised to hear from her, and suggested they call Joe to be a part of the meeting, making it less about the two of them and more about Jonathon.

"Good idea, I'll call Joe. See you soon."

An hour had passed, then there was a knock at the door. Sidney let the three of them in and led them to the dining room where Leslie had papers and her laptop on the table. After greeting each other, Leslie offered coffee and went to the kitchen.

"She has been busy," Annabelle said looking at some of the papers.

"Yes, and the more we delve into this, the clearer things appear," Sidney said. "And you know how she gets. She's like a bloodhound on the trail of a scent."

Leslie came back with cups and coffee. She poured each one a cup and sat down. "Before you lecture me, Annabelle, Sidney has said enough for both of you."

"I bet he has," Annabelle said shaking her head. "Now what's this theory of yours?"

"Okay, I started from the beginning of what we know. That was Margaret's antique clock."

"What?" Jeffrey said confused.

"Rose Marie said she introduced Margaret to Johnathon because Margaret wanted an antique clock repaired." Leslie explained.

"So, this involves Jonathon's clock repair shop?" Jeffrey said trying to keep up.

"Yes, so I called Rose Marie, who, by the way, confirmed my suspicions. All of you have said this was not like Jonathon and it was totally out of character. With that in mind, I tried to find a reason that explained his actions. In talking to Rose Marie, some things began to fall in place. She told me a couple of things that don't make sense. One being that Margaret told everyone on the Historic Committee that she didn't have children. She made such a big enough issue out of it that Rose Marie remembered her statement. Now, why would she lie about that? We now know that she indeed has a son."

"Who is her son?" Jeffrey asked trying to follow.

"After Leslie found him living right here in New Orleans, we put a tail on him. Once we were sure he was, in fact, her son, my agent Charles and I confronted him in an effort to find his mother," Sidney told Jeffrey.

"That's when Sidney found him in the act of breaking into his office, and before he escaped he hit Sidney over the head giving him a concussion," Annabelle said.

"Who are these people? And how is Jonathon mixed up with them," Jeffrey said frustrated.

"I agree, what's he involved in and with whom is he involved?" Joe said.

"Wait, there's more. One other thing that came out of my conversation with Rose Marie was when Doris was sick she took a covered dish over to their home and Margaret was there. When she asked Jonathon about it, he told her that Margaret had been helping him with Doris staying with her while he ran errands. That very night after Rose Marie discovered Margaret at the house, Doris died."

"What are you saying?" Annabelle asked.

"There's more. Rose Marie found out that Doris was dying when she saw Jonathon at the drugstore. He was getting a prescription filled for Doris. Rose Marie remembered it was a pain killer, not morphine, but Jonathon told her it was strong because Doris was in so much pain," Leslie said.

"So, you think those pain killers killed Doris? But she was dying. Wasn't it a natural death from the cancer?" Annabelle asked.

"Rose Marie said that Margaret was not at the funeral services for Doris. Being a friend, wouldn't you think she would be there?" Leslie asked. "But the nail in the coffin, so to speak, was when Rose Marie told me Margaret was absent at the next committee meeting, because her husband died."

"I'm lost. I don't get the connection," Annabelle said.

"Remember the newspaper article that Sidney found leading him to the identity of Margaret Trudeau? The article said her husband died of mysterious causes."

"Yes. I remember. But nothing else was ever said about that."

"Exactly. Why and who squelched that story? The so called mysterious death reported in the newspaper was never brought to light," Leslie was on a roll, now that her comrades were following her thought process. "Remembering my visit with attorney Trudeau, I was curious, if he said he ran a background check on Margaret before his son married her, then why had he not found the same information I discovered in researching her background? Just to keep everyone up to speed. I discovered Margaret had two previous husbands that were cremated shortly after their deaths. Didn't he find that information a little alarming when his son was also cremated soon after his death? And why would he not have shared his concern when I told him about Margaret's suspected criminal activity?"

"So, you thought Trudeau was hiding something?" Annabelle surmised.

Just then, Sidney's cell phone rang. He saw that it was Charles. Going to the other room, he answered.

"Sidney, we have movement, and I think mama is back in town."

"I'll call the police. You keep them in your sight. Don't lose them."

Back in the dining room, he told Annabelle that Margaret was at her son's house, and they were loading the car with suitcases.

"Did you call the police?" Annabelle said.

"I'm calling them right now." Sidney replied.

"I better call the DA's office, I know it is late, but Bryce may still be there."

Jeffrey was fascinated by the way Leslie, Sidney, and Annabelle worked. He had never been a part of this type of thing before and found it intriguing. The fact that his brother's life hung in the balance, and these three people were diligent in their efforts to save him, was almost overwhelming. He watched and listened intently, as Leslie wove the information into a scenario that was beginning to make sense.

He was not sure yet what this Trudeau guy and his brother had in common, but he knew Leslie was on the trail of something extremely important. When Sidney got a call from his agent, Charles, the information Leslie was sharing came to a standstill. It seemed, at this point, it was more important to apprehend the criminals. The knowledge that these people were dangerous took his breath away. He looked at Leslie and thought about their little boy. *How do they keep their cool knowing any minute things could go wrong?*

Only recently had Annabelle told him that Sidney was an FBI agent in his previous life before he fell in love with Leslie. *So, at least he has had training in this sort of thing*, he reassured himself. She also shared the story of her husband's murder, and how the three of them single-handedly solved that case. This was not the first time Leslie had put herself in danger in pursuit of the truth. So, for her to put herself in danger again seemed to be her mode of operation, throwing caution to the wind as she followed her intuition. He wondered if he could, like Sidney and Leslie, marry someone who lived on the edge so close to criminal activity. He was going to have to take his relationship with Annabelle more seriously as she could also put herself in danger as a criminal lawyer.

Chapter 31

Jonathon had not told Annabelle all the details of his relationship with Margaret. Guilt, shame, and disappointment encouraged the deletion of some very important information. He hoped she could build his defense on what he had given her. He gave her just enough of the story to be believable. *She's a good lawyer so what makes you think she won't find out more?* He asked himself.

He told Annabelle that Margaret had used him from the beginning, and he wasn't brave enough to put a stop to it. He told her that when he threatened to stop seeing Margaret, she made him feel guilty like she had done all those things for him and now he was just going to dump her. She gave him a sob story about how her husband had treated her and how broke she was and how she really loved him and how much she needed him.

Is Margaret hiding in Mexico like Sidney suggested? Will she come back? Or is this a big scam and I was the target all along? His pride was hoping at one point they had loved each other. She never loved you. She took you for a ride, and you let her. You're just kidding yourself, man. He accused himself. Hours spend with time to think, he was possessed by the fears that controlled his mind. His only hope was in the Lord, and that was what kept him going.

He put his head in his hands and began to talk to the only friend he had. *Oh Father, what have I done? Forgive me, Father, for the hurt I have caused my family, for my inflated ego. I wish I had been closer to You before all this happened. I'm not perfect, Jesus, but before this, I tried to be a good person, and I guess at first I thought I was still trying to be a good person. Thank you for Annabelle and Sidney. They have brought me back to You, and I know You're in control. Your word comforts me and gives me hope. I'm not sure why, but I pray for Margaret, I pray for her soul. I'm so ashamed for allowing her to manipulate me, Father. My prayer is that she will find you and ask for your forgiveness. I pray in Jesus' name. Amen.*

Chapter **32**

"Hurry up son, we haven't got all day. Someone could be watching us right now. We need to get on the road. We can't chance airports or rental cars, so we better hope your car will get us back to Mexico."

Margaret was street smart, but this time she was cutting it close, knowing they were on her trail. Once her son had botched the break-in of the Rye Agency, she knew she better get him back to Mexico where they would be safe. She wore another wig to hide her recognizable red hair. However, she felt that someone was watching her every move. She had worked too hard, too long to have things blow up now. The money accumulated over the death of three husbands was safely in the bank in Matamoras Mexico. Soon she and her son would be living a life of luxury just as she planned.

Putting the last suitcase in the trunk of the car, she slid into the driver's seat. "Son? Is this car in working order? No tail lights missing, nothing that would attract police?"

"No and I just filled the tank so we're good to go."

Margaret started to pull away from the curb when two squad cars, one in front and one in back blocked her.

"Everyone, out of the car." The officer told them.

*****

Charles and Sidney watched from a balcony across the street as the officers loaded the two into the squad cars. *Finally,* Sidney thought. *Now we can get to the bottom of this whole thing. And just maybe exonerate Jonathon in the process.*

Sidney called Leslie and told her the news. Annabelle, Jeffrey, and Joe were still there at the house, and Sidney said he would be there soon.

"I just got a call from the DA's office. They have our two fugitives in a holding cell at the county jail," Annabelle told Sidney on his arrival.

"Separately, I hope," Sidney said sitting down. "I'm surprised at how cooperative they were, especially Margaret. I guess she figured it would happen sooner or later."

"Do you think they were headed back to Mexico?" Leslie said.

"I would assume so. I'm guessing that was the plan all along," Sidney told Leslie.

"I wonder what Jonathon will say about this. I mean will he be glad Margaret has been caught?" Jeffrey said thinking out loud.

"It is only fair that she shares in this guilt. We still don't know the whole story. For that matter, we may never know. Shouldn't you call Rose Marie?" Leslie said to Jeffrey.

"Yes, Jeffrey maybe you should call her," Annabelle said.

"I was thinking you could call her Annabelle. She will want to know where I got the information. I really don't want her to think I'm doing anything behind her back," Jeffrey said. Then to Leslie and Sidney he said, "She doesn't know about me and Annabelle, yet."

"Why not?" Sidney said confused.

"Rose Marie wouldn't mind, in fact she would be happy for us and I'll tell her, but not now. She would think that Annabelle was keeping me informed about Jonathon's case and up until today that was not the case. My relationship with Annabelle has been personal, and she has never divulged her findings about Jonathon's situation."

"I see. Well, I would start confessing if I were you, because it's obvious to anyone around the two of you, that you're in love," Sidney smiled then winked at Leslie.

Jeffrey looked at Annabelle. "Our secret's out."

"Not funny, the three of you must be aware that we cannot be paired as a couple due to conflict of interest. So please, no more assuming remarks that people could overhear. We have to be really careful if I'm going to represent Jonathon."

"I'm sorry Annabelle, Jeffrey. How hard this must be for the two of you," Sidney said shaking his head, remembering how hard it was to keep secrets when he first met Leslie.

"Now that Margaret is in custody, maybe we can move this case along."

Chapter **33**

"Mrs. Trudeau, you have been read your rights, do you wish to make a statement?" Bryce asked.

Sitting across the table from the DA in a very bare, low-lit room, she weighed her options. She was sure now that Jonathon had spilled the beans, but the truth of the matter was, all he knew was the money end, and threats that no one could prove. So, she would have to be careful about anything she revealed. She hoped that her son could be cleared, and that would be her purpose going forward. The money was still in Mexico in the bank. She made sure her son could get the money if anything unforeseen happened by putting the account in his name. As soon as she arrived in New Orleans, she had him sign a signature card and immediately mailed it to the bank in Mexico. Even though he was not anxious to live in Mexico, Margaret assured him he would have a good life there.

"I believe, this is where I ask for a lawyer," she said smiling at the person she was sure wanted to nail her to the wall with his inquiries.

"You could save us all a lot of time if you would just tell us your side of the story," he replied.

"That will be up to my lawyer," she said.

"So, do you have a lawyer, or do we assign you a public defender?"

"I think Shelby Trudeau would be happy to take my case," she said with a smirk on her face.

"THE Shelby Trudeau? Your ex-father-in-law?"

"That would be he. So, Mr. District Attorney, why don't you give him a call?"

*****

With his hand still on the receiver, his face went ashen and his breathing became labored. He had hoped she would never come back to the states. *If only she had stayed in Mexico,* he thought. *Why did she come back? How did she get caught? Most of all, why me? Why does she think I could defend her?* His heart was pounding out of his chest just thinking about the ramifications of the widow of his son being incarcerated. He was convinced she had something to do with his son's death. Now his reputation was on the line. Was the past about to catch up with him?

He reached for the phone and dialed a number etched in his memory.

"Hello Marcus, how have you been?"

"I'm doing okay Shelby, how are you?"

"Well, I was doing pretty well until my son got mixed up with that cougar."

"How is Margaret nowadays?" Marcus asked.

"She wants me to be her attorney. To defend her of all things."

"Defend her against what?"

"Well, it's a long story, and I don't know the whole story, but the parts I do know would make your hair stand on end, that's if you have any hair."

"No, Shelby, I'm as bald as you are. However, my head has a better shape. So why are you calling me?"

"I need you to find something I can use on our lady friend. Some dirt, if you will. Start with those other two husbands of hers. There is another PI nosing around in this, and I think they may have found something."

"Why's there a PI involved in this?"

"It seems that our cougar was in bed with this poor guy and managed to help him embezzle his family's trust fund. The guy has been in jail for the last few months. Now his partner, our Margaret, and her son, have been arrested on the same charges."

"Embezzlement? That's a new venue for her and since when does she have a son? I always thought her game was marrying kids you know Harold must have been at least 15 years her junior not much older than any kids she could have."

"Oh, I'm sure there are many things we do not know about her, but I intend to find out, that's why I want to hire you. You will be up against a pretty sharp PI, I understand he used to be an FBI agent," Shelby said.

"I think I can handle it. By the way, what ever happened to the charges you were going to bring against her? Didn't you have some proof that she was involved in Harold's death?" Marcus asked.

Shelby was silent as he contemplated the answer to that question. Then not wanting to reveal his motive, he told Marcus he was wrong. After investigating the cause of Harold's death, he didn't have enough evidence to convict, so he dropped it and persuaded the newspaper to stop the story. He wasn't sure Marcus bought it, but for now he had bigger things on his mind.

"Okay, I'll do some digging and get back with you. Just like 'ole times.'"

"Yeah, dig deep man, pull in all your favors," Shelby said and hung up.

*****

"Well now, Shelby, we find ourselves in a real dilemma. I've heard you're an excellent criminal lawyer. So, let's see how good you really are. First of all, I want out of here as soon as possible," Margaret said with the utmost confidence.

"That's not going to happen. You're a flight risk. You've been on their radar too long for them to let you out on bond. Remember, you were the one who took off to Mexico," Shelby said.

"I'm the one calling the shots, and if you want to keep that precious reputation of yours you'll pull in some favors and get me out of here, understood?" She said leaning across the table.

"I understand your son is being detained. It would be a real shame if he found out his mother got out, and he had to stay in jail for a trial. I'm sure hoping he's not involved in this scam of yours. He probably doesn't even know how deep the water is where you're standing. My guess is, he is just a puppet doing what mommy tells him."

"You leave my son out of this. He is probably out by now anyway. Jonathon couldn't possibly have implemented him in this."

"I think he is being held as a coconspirator which means…"

"I know what it means," Margaret said then leaned back in her chair staring into Shelby's face. Her mouth was shut tight with her jaw set solid. Her eyelids were almost covering her eyes. Then she took a big breath and said, "What are you suggesting?"

"Who me? Why, I'm not suggesting anything. I'm just telling you what's going on with your son. But, I think you would be wise to think about a few things before you start giving me orders. You're in deep water lady, and if you and your son plan to have any kind of future, you had better get your act together. Like you said I'm an excellent criminal lawyer," Shelby exclaimed getting up from his chair and lifting his briefcase from the table. "And by the way, I haven't committed to being your attorney yet. Guard."

"Aren't you forgetting something?"

"No. But you are. I know what happened to my son," Shelby said leaving the room. He was well aware that representing his ex-daughter-in-law would be a conflict of interest, but that information wouldn't be available to Margaret yet while he fished for details to use against her.

Leaving the jail, he decided to visit the Rye agency.

"Hello Sidney. How are things going with your business?"

"Real well Shelby, and yours," Sidney said pointing to a chair.

"Can't complain. Funny thing though, Margaret Trudeau wants me to be her attorney. Can you believe that?" he said sitting down across from Sidney. "I just came from talking to her. By the way, your wife is quite the investigator."

Sidney decided to be silent and see if Shelby would tip his hand. The more he talked the more it became obvious he was trying to pull information out of Sidney, but it wasn't working. After all this wasn't Sidney's first rodeo. Years as an FBI agent testifying before the government gave him a heads up on interrogation technology. After a few minutes he began to feel sorry for the guy and asked if he knew much about Margaret's son.

"I didn't even know she had a son. I don't think Harold did either."

"We sure didn't know."

"I'm really in a predicament here, man, you know what I mean. If you know anything I can use to get out of this I would appreciate it."

"You're a smart lawyer, I'm sure you'll figure it out. Now I have to get busy. Sorry I can't be of any help," Sidney said getting up and offering his hand.

Shelby got up, shook Sidney's hand and left the office. Sidney immediately called Leslie. "Les, your favorite male attorney was just here. It seems Margaret is wanting him to represent her."

"Wow, I bet that made him wiggle. What did he want from you?"

"Information."

"See, my theory is right. I wonder what he is going to do. Do you think he will represent her?"

"He didn't sound like that was his plan, and honestly I don't think he can represent her even if he wanted to. I think he is behind the eight ball. I almost felt sorry for him."

"I know. Even when he was ushering me out of his office, and as scared as I was, I still couldn't help but feel sorry for him."

"He said that he nor Harold knew she had a son."

"Well, that's interesting."

"I better let you get back to your research and I'll do some more leg work. Maybe we can crack this case. I love you. See you tonight."

Chapter **34**

A nnabelle realized because of her involvement with Jeffrey, she may have to excuse herself as Jonathon's Attorney. She was mulling this possibility over in her mind when Sidney called and told her about the visit from Trudeau.

"Sidney, do you think he would help with Jonathon's case?" she said after telling him of her dilemma. "This would solve his problem and mine too. I think I could convince Jonathon."

"But wouldn't Trudeau have the same conflict, since Margaret was his daughter-in-law?" Sidney said.

"He wouldn't be representing her. Actually, he would be implementing her."

"How sweet for him."

"Maybe he could be working on the team for Jonathon's defense and at the same time implementing Margaret. I would think that would attract him to the cause, since Margaret probably took his son for big bucks, too."

"You have never said exactly what Jonathon has told you, but I have always had the feeling there's more to the story than even you know."

"Yes, that's been my feeling all along, so I'm thinking Trudeau could possibly fill in the blanks," Annabelle told Sidney. "I think I'll give Shelby a call and feel him out, let's see what he's got in mind."

*****

Rose Marie sat stoic, staring at the TV screen. The image of Margaret and her son being removed from the police cars was surreal. *How could this woman, a liar be involved with my brother? What has she gotten him involved in?* Her head was spinning trying to sort things out. *Nothing makes any sense, not Jonathon being accused of embezzlement, not his involvement with Margaret, obviously old enough to be his mother or close to it, and not the fact she lied about having children, probably Jonathon's age. It just doesn't seem real.*

Patrick watched his wife, as the look on her face went from disbelief to anger to sorrow. The tears rolled down her face staining her blouse. He got up and sat beside her. Taking her hand, he began to ask God for peace and strength to see them through. She laid her head on his shoulder trying to stop the agony she felt.

"Does Jonathon know she's been arrested?" she asked.

"I don't know. I would assume he does. I just don't know, honey."

"I wonder if he turned her in."

"Quite possibly," Patrick said.

"If he did, was it to save his own skin, or did he suddenly get a conscience?" she said still leaning on Patrick's shoulder. "Were they lovers? Oh Patrick, she's so much older. That wouldn't make much difference if she was a good woman, but I just don't understand what he saw in her."

Patrick didn't answer. He had his own thoughts rambling around in his head, thoughts he didn't want to share with his wife. He had thought from the beginning there was something strange going on, but because he had no information to back up his theories he didn't voice his ideas. He had known Jonathon for many years and never saw this criminal side of him, and that's what made it so hard to accept this character flaw. Jonathon would have to be crazy or trapped before he would knowingly participate in any wrongdoing. The several times Patrick visited him in jail he was taken back by Jonathon's peace. He knew Jonathon was reading the Bible and praying, but this was more an attitude of relief or peace, like a belief that he would get through this on the right side of the law.

"Come on, let's go to bed," Patrick said lifting Rose Marie's head from his shoulder. "Things always look better in the morning."

Chapter **35**

Before she could have a conversation with Shelby Trudeau, she needed to talk to Jonathon. Staring at the door waiting for the guard to bring Jonathon to the room where they could talk, her brain went into overload. She had to convince him to come clean and tell her everything or his defense could not happen. Her own emotions put aside, she wanted Jonathon to have the best defense she could offer, and that wouldn't happen if he held back on important information.

"Hello Annabelle," Jonathon said sitting down across from her.

"Jonathon," she said calmly.

"Sidney told me they have arrested Margaret and her son," he said.

"Yes, that's why I'm here and I really need all the information you can give me, if you want me to go forward with your defense," she said sternly.

"I've told you what happened," Jonathon said adjusting himself in the chair.

"Jonathon, this is serious. If you can't be honest with me and trust me then I may have to excuse myself as your attorney."

Shaking his head, he lowered his eyes and said a silent prayer before telling her the whole story, this time not leaving anything out.

After he left the room, she sat at the table going over her notes. Some of what he disclosed she already suspected, but when he revealed the bottom line of their volatile relationship, she tried to console him and told him she would do everything in her power to set him free, and make sure Margaret stayed behind bars the rest of her life.

*****

Shelby Trudeau agreed to meet with Annabelle at her office because she wanted to be on her own turf, remembering her many times on the opposite side in court she knew his tactics, so when his immense body stood in the doorway, she braced herself for the conversation ahead.

"Hello Shelby, have a seat," she said extending her hand.

"Nice office, Ms. Robicheaux," he said looking around. "It shows that you must be good at this law thing to be able to afford the luxury of such expensive things."

Ignoring his remark, not allowing his flattering to deter her purpose for their meeting or giving him a chance to put her off guard, she thanked him then got right to the point. "I'm sure you know I represent Jonathon Bordeaux and I'm aware that Margaret Trudeau has been arrested for her involvement in the embezzlement of the Bordeaux Family Trust."

"This is true," he said curious as to why he was here.

"I would like to propose that we work together on my case, letting you off the hook so to speak. Because I understand Margaret wants you to represent her, and beside the fact that since she was your daughter-in-law you can't represent her, this may give you a chance to set the record straight."

Annabelle's Hollywood beauty had Shelby's full attention. Contemplating working with her, increased his pulse rate, but, chastising himself, he came back to reality. With a look of concern, he stared past her trying to figure out his next move knowing he had to pick his words carefully. She watched as he began tapping his puffy fingers on the wooden arms of the leather chair as his nostrils flared, revealing his deep breathing, expanding his oversized chest. He asked her for a glass of water and watched her retrieve the water from a pitcher on the credenza behind her desk revealing her shapely body as she turned and set the glass in front of him.

"Well, little lady, that's a fine proposal. However, it may be difficult for us to work together on the same side knowing our history and all, so what makes you think this would be a good match?"

"I believe you want Margaret behind bars as much as I do. And, you may unknowingly possess information pertinent to Jonathon's case because you're aquatinted with her mode of operation, since she was married to your son. Much against your wishes, am I right?"

"You could have a point there. However, I think by playing along with her, letting her think I can represent her, I'll be able to gain some leverage,"

"What about client privilege? It could hurt my case if she told you facts under the impression that you were her attorney, have you thought about that?"

"As a matter of fact, I have. She's convinced that I can pull strings and get her out just like that and to be honest, I know how devious she can be, and it wouldn't take much for her to turn her wrath on me in some way if you know what I mean," Shelby said not revealing the fact she may have something on him.

"So, Shelby, are you declining my offer?"

Getting his bulky body up from the chair, he offered his hand, then told her he would need to think about it, and to give him 24 hours to make a decision. She shook his hand, noticing he held hers a little too long, then accepted his time frame, encouraging him to not take any longer than 24 hours.

After he left, Annabelle mulled their conversation over in her mind pausing on his remark about Margaret's wrath turning on him indicating as Leslie had surmised, she had something on him but what? They already knew about the scrapes Harold got into in college, was there something more serious that happened and if so, did Margaret know about it? On a hunch, she carefully picked up the glass Shelby drank from and placed it in a zip locked bag then she called Leslie.

Chapter **36**

After Annabelle's call, Leslie began to delve more deeply into Harold Trudeau's volatile days in college starting with his fraternity brothers. She looked up the roster of the fraternity in the years he belonged and, one by one began to check their records. Several, like Harold, had gotten into scrapes with the law but unlike Harold, some were expelled or worse, served jail time or community service. Starting the last year, Harold was in the fraternity she was surprised to learn that the first name on the list was Jason Anderson, an upperclassman. Could it be the same Jason Anderson, son of Margaret Anderson Trudeau?

Sure enough, they were one in the same and not only that, Jason and Harold were roommates. *How interesting is that?* Leslie thought as she continued to search for any record of Jason being in jail or any criminal activity that he and Harold may have been involved in. Then there it was Jason was expelled from the university for a hazing incident that also implicated Harold but evidently Daddy got Harold out of trouble and Jason had to pay the price.

So, Trudeau did know about Margaret's son after all, because Jason and Harold were roommates. No wonder he was concerned when Harold married Margaret who was eighteen or twenty years older and the mother of his son's friend Jason. So why did she marry Harold? To get back at his daddy for her son being expelled or was there something else going on. Leslie continued to speculate without anything firm to go by.

She wanted a copy of the Chronicle Newspaper at the University that came out about the same time as the hazing incident. Searching through page after page, finally an article caught her eye. *You don't suppose this has anything to do with anything?* She wondered to herself and picking up her cell phone, she called Sidney.

"Whoa, Les, slow down. I can't follow you," Sidney said aware that Leslie had stumbled onto something important. "Wait, shouldn't Annabelle hear this too? Okay, let's get together. I'll call Annabelle, and we will meet you at the house in say thirty minutes."

Sidney and Annabelle arrived at the same time and hurried up the steps to the front door that Leslie held open for them.

"This is the answer we have been waiting for guys. This is the missing part of the puzzle." Leslie squealed.

"Enough, what is it?" Annabelle said sitting at the table across from Leslie.

She told them what she found out about Harold and Jason, and she concluded that she thought that was the reason Margaret somehow convinced Harold to marry her.

"But what did she have on Shelby, and what did it have to do with Jason and Harold?" Sidney said anxiously.

"Oh, how convenient for Margaret to find someone like Jonathon, newly widowed, executor of a family trust, to weave her wicked web to snare him. He didn't have a chance," Annabelle said.

"Okay, this is what I think is behind all of this. In the Chronicle Newspaper at the University around the time the boys were in trouble for the hazing incident there was another event. A young lady was reported missing after a frat party, you guessed it, the same fraternity the boys belonged too. In another article in the same Newspaper a week or so later, her body was found in Lake Pontchartrain right here in New Orleans near the causeway. Since we have already established Shelby's recue of his son when he was in trouble, this could be the very thing Margaret is holding over his head. She could have proof of his son's involvement in this girl's disappearance," Leslie announced breathlessly, wheels turning faster in her mind than she could keep up with.

"So, how do we connect the girl with Harold?" Jonathon's attorney asked in need of proof.

"I think I have a clue. After talking to some of the frat brothers, I discovered that Harold and Jason had dated this same girl, and Jason brought her to the party the night she disappeared."

"And the plot thickens. Oh Leslie, good work. Sidney, we have to figure out how to make Jason talk about this girl. Any ideas?"

"Not at the moment." Still reeling from the information, Sidney was working things out in his mind. "So, Les, you think that the boys somehow dropped her off the causeway into the lake?"

"Oh, and I think the autopsy report will show she drowned but not in the lake. What if the autopsy showed chlorine was present."

"That would be a piece of news we definitely need. So, the girl could have drowned somewhere at the university, and then her body was put in the lake." Annabelle said.

"Exactly!" Leslie said leaning back in her chair with hands clasps behind her head in triumph.

"Wait a minute mystery solver, that doesn't explain what Margaret is holding over Jonathon," Sidney said winking at Leslie.

"I think I know the answer to that, but we need to tie up some loose ends, so we can go to trial which, by the way, is coming up soon," Annabelle told them.

Chapter **37**

"What do you mean that's the only information? The Rye Agency has a plethora of information about her, and the only thing you found was she was pregnant in high school. What does that have to do with anything?" Shelby shouted into the phone.

"Wait a minute boss, and I'll tell you the connection. Margaret had a baby boy when she was eighteen. Here's the kicker, his name is Jason, Jason Anderson to be exact," Marcus said sternly.

"So, is that supposed to mean something to me?"

"It should since Jason was your son's roommate in college."

Silent as he absorbed this information. Margaret's son was a roommate of my son Harold. Wait a minute. So that is why she hates me so. Jason was expelled from the university, and I managed to keep Harold out of trouble. He thought. But what else does she know?

"Good work, Marcus. Let's keep in touch," he said ending the phone call before Marcus started asking questions. The less he knew, the better and right now Shelby's concern for his own skin was heightened by this information, and he had better get to work before his life as he knew it came crashing down around him.

Why didn't I know that Margaret was Jason's mother? Why didn't Harold know that? Well, I guess that is not impossible since I never met this Jason character when he was Harold's roommate, so it is possible Harold never met Jason's Mother. They could have very well dreamed this scam up to get back at me. But why get rid of Harold? Could it be that Harold knew more about Jason's involvement than even I knew? When Margaret threatened me with exposure, I thought she meant the hazing incident. That's before I knew about her son Jason. She said Harold had spilled the beans about his college days one night in a drunken state.

Should I go to Annabelle and plead for mercy? They are sure to discover this piece of information soon and then where will I be? All the things he did for his only son, then to lose him in the end, weighed on him as he tried to figure out what steps to take. Just then the phone rang giving him a jolt.

"Trudeau."

"Hello Shelby, since I didn't hear from you I'm assuming you don't want to be part of Jonathon's defense team?" Annabelle said.

"Oh, hello Annabelle, you're right, I'm sorry I didn't call you earlier. I just don't think my involvement would help your case," he said barely able to keep his thoughts together as he tried to sound convincing.

"Shelby, are you alright? You don't sound like yourself. Is everything okay? Have you seen Margaret again? Does she still want you to represent her? Has she got something on you to make you consider taking her case even if you could? What's going on

Shelby?" Annabelle said as she threw a barrage of question at him in rapid secession. Then she asked in her most sincere voice. "Do you need a lawyer?"

He could feel his blood pressure rise as anger took over then he said with venom in his words. "No, I don't need a lawyer, I AM a lawyer. What did you mean by that?"

"Well, Shelby, we have run across some interesting tidbits that could put you in the need of a good attorney," she answered in a low calming voice.

"I don't know what you are talking about, Ms. Robicheaux," he said barely able to speak above a whisper.

"I see. Well then, I guess I misjudged the situation you find yourself in, I apologize. However, I would cross your t's and dot your i's going forward if I were you, so you don't run into any trouble. Goodbye Shelby," she said ending the conversation before he could reply.

Her hand still on the phone she had a pain of sympathy for Shelby but remembering what Leslie had uncovered, it only lasted for a second. She was now convinced that Shelby was involved in that girl's disappearance, but how involved was he? She knew he bailed Harold out of first one mess then another, but this was a bigger mess than she had bargained for. How was she going to piece it together unless she had Shelby's help? She was sure Jonathon knew nothing about Jason which would certainly help his case.

Chapter **38**

Entering her home, Annabelle felt a sense of dread, the uneasy feeling that something wasn't right causing anxious thoughts to surround her. Because there were still missing pieces to the puzzle, she realized she still had her work cut out for her. *But, how am I going to convince a jury that Jonathon is innocent when all the evidence points in his direction?* Knowing how Leslie's mind worked weaving in and out of her stories she called her.

"Hello."

"Hi Leslie, it's me. Do you have time for me to run some things by you?"

"Sure, what's going on?"

"I think I am in overload with all the information and I just need you to help me sort some things out."

"Do you want to come over, Daisy is getting ready to put Ryan down for a nap," Leslie told her.

Waiting for Annabelle to arrive Leslie made an outline of the facts as she knew them putting each fact beside the name of the person in the puzzle starting with Harold and Jason, roommates in college involved but never implicated in the disappearance of a girl they had both dated. Then there was Harold's father who knew how the law worked and seemingly managed to protect his son Harold. Jason, however, was expelled from the University for his involvement in a hazing incident. Margaret, Jason's mother, for reasons unknown except for her son being expelled, started a journey of revenge.

Annabelle exhausted from trying to figure things out and a little frustrated at not being able to see Jeffrey, she gathered her stacks of paper and put them in her briefcase then went down the steps and through the walkway to the gate. Walking toward Jackson Square, she hailed a taxi and headed for the Garden District. Arriving a few moments later she climbed the steps to Leslie's home and rang the doorbell. Leslie let her in and the two of them headed for the dining room table where Leslie had her notes and laptop.

"Okay, I'm here, let's figure this thing out," Annabelle said opening her briefcase and laying her papers on the case, in front of her.

Leslie showed her the outline and asked if anything was missing. Annabelle told her, as far as she knew from the information she had, it was accurate.

"Don't you feel it, Leslie? We are missing something. What else would drive someone like Margaret to make such an elaborate plan of revenge? Did you find anything else in your research that would answer that question?" Annabelle said.

"Before we go any further Annabelle let's ask God to help us."

Holding each other's hands, they bowed their heads in prayer. *Father, to you be the glory, and we praise you in everything we do.*

Thank you for your faithfulness, God. We are so blessed by your sacrifice, your gift of salvation. We ask for your guidance in this mystery that we may help those involved. In Jesus' name. Amen

"Thank you, Leslie."

They continued to share information looking for a clue into Margaret's motive. By this time, it was becoming clear that Margaret did have something to do with Harold's death. It was also clear Shelby Trudeau knew more than he was revealing about Margaret and his son Harold.

"Why can't we see it, Leslie?"

"Don't give up Annabelle, we are both good at research and it is bound to be here, right in front of us, and we will find it," Leslie said a little frustrated herself but not wanting Annabelle to get discouraged. "Wait a minute, here is something we've overlooked before," Leslie said looking at the screen on her laptop.

"What?"

"Shelby graduated from the same high school that Margaret went to. Now, how's that for a coincident? He was a couple of years ahead of her but Annabelle, the same high school."

"Maybe that's why Shelby's been so coy. Maybe what Margaret has on him goes way back. But what could she have on him and why now?

"Think about it, Leslie. Just for conversation's sake, say Jason told his mother about the girl disappearing and what happened to her. Right? Then, that is what she was holding over Shelby's head, but her revenge went further than that."

"Yes." Leslie asked confused, "and what does it have to do with Jonathon?"

"It could have been a convenience, a way for her to secure her and her son's future, knowing everything about what happened when the boys were in college," Annabelle said.

"Well, this certainly puts a new light on things. Now what?" Leslie said getting up from the chair and stretching. "How about some coffee? I'll make it while you keep churning thoughts in that brain of yours," Leslie said heading for the kitchen.

Coming back to the dining room Leslie said. "So, you think Margaret knew how vulnerable Jonathon was and…. wait a minute. Remember the painkillers Jonathon got for Doris? That is the loose end I was trying to tie up. Do you think Margaret got her hands on the painkillers after or even before Doris died and used them to kill Harold? I thought about that a while back before the police arrested Margaret and her son."

"It certainly goes along with what Jonathon told me, which was that all the things he eventually did were because Margaret threatened to implicate him in Harold's death."

"You mean she actually confessed to killing Harold?"

"Inferred it, to keep Jonathon doing what she wanted. I don't think there is enough proof to charge her with murder unless Jonathon's story can convince a jury. Which reminds me, I better get to work on his defense, especially with new information to help his case."

After another cup of coffee, Annabelle gave Leslie a hug and called for a taxi.

"Thanks, Leslie, I knew you could help with this puzzle," Annabelle said when the taxi came.

On the ride back to her office, she went over in her mind the information she and Leslie had discovered. There was still more to this story than was revealed however she had some ideas she didn't share with Leslie. If what she was thinking was true, then her case for Jonathon was about to take a serious turn.

Chapter **39**

The courtroom was packed with the Bordeaux family, friends Leslie Sidney, Joe and Sadie Sully and curious onlookers. Jonathon sat at the defense table next to Annabelle waiting for the bailiff to announce the entrance of the Judge.

"All rise, the Honorable Judge Mary Chase residing,"

Judge Chase had gone to law school with Annabelle and allowed no nonsense in her courtroom. She began to give strict instruction to the jury that was selected the day before. Calling on the prosecution, then the defense, for opening statements as the trail of Jonathon Bordeaux began.

After a short recess to allow their defense witness to come from the jail, under guard, Annabelle began her interrogation. She first established connection between Jason and Margaret that he was Margaret's son, then she asked Jason if he knew the defendant. He answered no.

"Did Margaret ever tell you about her relationship with Jonathon?"

"No."

"Did you ever meet Jonathon?"

"No."

"Did she ever tell you about Jonathon's family, his boat, anything about him at all?"

"She told me she was in a relationship with a very wealthy man? But I didn't know who it was. She did tell me about the boat, and said one day she would take me out and show me how to sail."

"In the eight months, your mother was married did she ever talk about this wealthy man and his boat."

"No."

"Did you ever meet any of your mother's friends?"

"No. She was somewhat of a social climber, on committees and such and she did volunteer work."

"What kind of volunteer work?"

"She told me about this couple she was helping. The wife had cancer and was dying, and the husband had repaired her antique clock. She was taking food and staying with the wife while the husband ran errands."

"Thank you, Mr. Anderson," Annabelle said then turning to the Judge, "that's all for this witness at this time but I reserve the right to recall him at a later date."

"This witness is incarcerated in the city jail do you wish him to return to jail and be brought back for further questioning?"

"Yes, your honor if it pleases the court."

*****

Originally in court to support his brother, now his whole being was focused on Attorney Annabelle Robicheaux. Jeffrey sat in awe watching Annabelle at work as she skillfully pulled information from each witness with the right questions for the answers that helped her case. To see her as an attorney at work gave him a clearer picture of who she was as a person. This other side of her, skill, knowledge and the ability to put it to use intrigued Jeffrey.

It was unbearable to avoid being with her the past few weeks and seeing her now brought all the feelings of pride, contentment and love he felt for her, to the forefront. His pulse rate increased at the sight of her, but he knew how important it was to keep his desires in check for his brother's sake.

Her interrogation of Jason captivated him as he wondered where it was leading. The mention of the couple Margaret took care of opened an avenue for further investigation. Jeffrey watched his brother Jonathon when Annabelle asked Jason questions and realized the agony he must be enduring thru all the questions. *Somehow, he must know she played him,* Jeffrey thought, *but why did she get away with it was the real question?*

The court reconvened after lunch and everyone came back in the courtroom and took their seats. Rose Marie leaned over and asked Jeffrey how he thought it was going and he answered, "so far, so good".

"I call Jonathon Bordeaux to the stand," Annabelle said.

All eyes were on him as he laid his hand on the bible and swore to tell the truth then he sat down in the chair and for the first time was face-to-face with his family. He took a cleansing breath and silently said a prayer. *Father be with me, help me be factual and tell the truth even if it exposes my sins Lord. I pray in the name of Jesus Christ. Amen.*

Annabelle began to weave the pattern of Margaret's deception as question after question ended with Jonathon obeying Margaret's every command.

"Jonathon, I know this is hard for you, but would you tell us why you did Margaret's bidding?"

"One day after I bought the boat and drained the bank account and the line of credit against the family home that was in the trust, I realized it wasn't going to end and I was not going to be able to pay any of it back. I felt like a fool and wanted it to be over, so I could make amends. I told Margaret our relationship had to end. and she told me I'd better think twice about that because she would tell the police we were lovers before her husband died and we planned to kill him together, but I couldn't wait and I killed him with the prescription painkillers my wife used before she died and that is why she had her husband's body cremated to protect me." Jonathon said, not looking at anyone in his family.

"I couldn't believe my ears. I didn't know what to do. I was really afraid of her at that point because she was very convincing. She had been to my house helping with my wife Doris when she was dying of cancer, so she could easily say we were having an affair."

"Were you having an affair with Margaret while your wife Doris was dying, and Margaret was married to Harold Trudeau?"

"No. She started out being a client when I fixed her Antique clock. Then we became friends when she was helping take care of my wife Doris. I appreciated her help, but we never were more than friends at that point."

"When did the relationship change?"

"Several weeks after her husband died, she called me. I was lonely and quite honestly had missed our friendship. We started talking about our grief on the phone, then we had dinner a couple of times. From there it became a romance."

"Were you in love with her?"

"I thought I was at one time but after she threatened me the romance was gone. I just became her slave."

"One more thing Jonathon, as a friend did she come to Doris's memorial services?"

"No."

"Did she tell you why she wasn't there?"

"Something about her husband not feeling well."

"Thank you, Jonathon that is all. Your witness," she said turning to the prosecution table.

"In light of the time, your honor, I have no questions but reserve the right to question at a later date," the prosecutor said, and the judge dismissed Jonathon and told the jury they would be held in a hotel overnight until the court convened the next day.

When Annabelle turned to talk to Jonathon before he went back to his cell, she caught a glimpse of Shelby Trudeau as he snuck out of the court room.

*****

Back in court the next day Annabelle looked around to make sure her other witness was in the courtroom.

After taking the stand, Annabelle asked Jason, "Did you know Margaret's deceased husband, Harold Trudeau?"

Jason didn't answer. Taking a deep breathe he said, "I knew him in college. We were roommates."

"Did you know he was married to your mother?"

"Not until after he died," Jason said, confused.

"Did you know Harold's father, Shelby Trudeau?"

"I knew of him; his name was always in the paper. He's a lawyer."

"But you never met him personally?"

"No."

"Not even when you and his son were in college together sharing a room and being fraternity brothers?"

Just then the prosecutor stood and voiced an objection.

"Overruled," the judge said.

"Are you sure you never met Shelby Trudeau."

"No, I never met him."

"Jason why were you expelled, one semester before earning your degree from the University?"

"I don't remember."

"Did it have something to do with a hazing incident?"

"I don't remember."

"Do you remember why Harold wasn't expelled for the same incident?"

"Yeah, his father pulled some strings and got him out of the charges," Jason said with anger.

"Did Harold's father ever help you out of a sticky situation?"

"No."

"According to records, there was an incident that occurred around the same time as the hazing incident, involving a girl that went missing. Do you remember that incident?"

"Your honor, where is this going?" the prosecutor asked.

"Ms. Robicheaux?" the judge asked.

"We want to establish the motive your honor."

"Continue, but be careful," the judge warned.

"Thank you, your honor. Mr. Anderson, do you remember the case of a girl who went to a fraternity party and later her body turned up in Lake Ponchartrain, dead from supposed drowning?"

"Yes."

"Did you, in fact, know this girl?"

"Yes."

"In fact, didn't you take her to the previously mentioned fraternity party?"

"I think so, I can't remember?"

"Did Harold Trudeau also know this girl?"

"Yes, I think so."

"Were you aware she didn't actually drown in the lake, but in a pool?"

"No," Jason said while adjusting himself in the chair.

"We have no further questions at this time but would ask that Mr. Anderson stay in the courtroom for now, so we can recall him later."

The courtroom was quiet while Jason was shown to a seat with a guard by his side. Annabelle asked if she could approach the bench.

"Your honor, I would like to call a witness not on the list."

"I will allow it," the judge said after a nod from the prosecutor.

"I call Shelby Trudeau to the stand," she said looking out over the courtroom.

For a split second, Shelby looked at the door for an escape, but with guards at each door decided not to try anything. All eyes were on him as he slowly walked to the stand.

After being sworn in, he put his oversized body in the chair, adjusting his suit coat, then looked at Annabelle, as he waited for her first question.

"Mr. Trudeau, do you know Jason Anderson, son of your ex-daughter-in-law, Margaret Trudeau?"

"Can't say that I do," he answered with a smirk as he looked at the jury.

"Are you now aware that Jason Anderson was your son Harold's roommate, and they belonged to the same fraternity, which by the way was also your fraternity?"

"I guess so, I don't see that it matters," he said again looking at the jury.

"Mr. Trudeau, answer the questions without comments," the judge instructed.

"Yes, your honor," he said.

"What was your relationship with his mother Margaret Anderson Trudeau?"

"She married my son, Harold."

"How did you feel about that?"

"What do you mean, how did I feel?"

"Did you know Margaret Anderson before she married your son?"

"No."

"Are you sure about that?"

"Yes, I am sure about that."

"Didn't the two of you attend the same high school?"

"How would I know?"

"Were you aware she gave birth to her son Jason when she was a senior in the same High School you graduated from a couple of years before?"

"Where is this going, Ms. Robicheaux? And what has it got to do with the embezzlement charges against your client?" he said in a loud accusative voice.

"Careful Mr. Trudeau, you are a witness, so answer the question," Judge Chase said, firmly.

"Okay, no I didn't know she got pregnant and had a son in high school," he replied with great sarcasm.

"Before this trial began, Jason Anderson agreed to a DNA test. The results came back that gives Margaret a more serious reason for trapping my client into her scheme."

"Do tell," Shelby retorted.

"Do you remember at my invitation, coming to my office to discuss my client's trial?"

"I do."

"I offered you a glass of water at that meeting. After you left I had preserved that glass with your DNA. After obtaining Mr. Anderson's DNA, I had your DNA tested. You see Mr. Trudeau that test proves you are the father of Jason Anderson and Margaret, his mother has been plotting her revenge against you for many years." Gasps and whispers filled the room.

"Quiet. Anymore commotion and I will have each of you removed from the courtroom," Judge Chase said, banging her gavel.

"Jason and Harold are, or were, half-brothers. When the two of them got into trouble in college, you made sure Harold didn't pay the price. Around that time, Harold wanted to protect Jason when the girl he had brought to the fraternity party accidentally drowned in the pool. Again, you came to the rescue. You helped Harold dump the body in the lake. Harold didn't want Jason to be blamed, so you and Harold came up with the plan. If you let Jason take the fall for the hazing incident, he wouldn't be implicated in the girl's disappearance. And, Margaret married Harold for the sole purpose of revenge. She hated you and Harold for letting Jason take the blame."

"I think you will agree, that your DNA has proven not only that you are Jason's father, but you withheld information. Do you remember the news story you managed to stop about the cause of your son's death? Did Margaret threaten you with information she heard from Harold, when he was drunk, implicating you in the case of the missing girl?"

"That is all speculation, Ms. Robicheaux, only one problem, you can't prove a word of it, and you know it. You are on a fishing expedition," Shelby said with sweat dripping from his brow.

"Margaret Trudeau has confessed to killing your son, Harold, and has told us what he told her. Jason can fill in the blanks, Mr.

Trudeau, so the DA has all they need to move on with an indictment. Do you have anything further you wish to say? You know the drill, anything you say can be held against you."

Shelby shook his head as the bailiff came forward took his arm and walked with him toward the courtroom door. Jason watched as the father he never knew was being escorted out of the room. Just then Shelby stopped and turned to look at him, his son, the son Margaret never told him about. The son he got expelled for college preventing him from graduating. The son he put on a path of destruction. Tears welled up on his eyelids then he turned and walked out of the courtroom to the waiting sheriff.

Looking at the defense table, Judge Chase asked Jonathon and Annabelle to stand. "In light of everything we have learned during this trial, and the fact your client turned state's witness leading to a confession by Margaret Trudeau in the death of Harold. The jury is dismissed. Thank you for your service. On the recommendation of the prosecution, I, therefore, sentence, the defendant, Jonathon Bordeaux, to ten years' probation and during the same said ten-year period to make financial reparation to the heirs of the Bordeaux Family Trust.

"In the matter of Shelby Trudeau, I will recommend he be brought before the Bar Association on charges of misconduct in the duties of upholding the law. If found guilty he will be disbarred which means unable to practice law in the state of Louisiana.

"Concerning Jason Anderson, he will be brought up for trial in the charges of breaking and entering, and assault resulting in injury."

"Thank you, your honor," Annabelle said.

"Court is dismissed."

Jonathan bowed his head in thanksgiving, *"Thank you, Jesus, thank You, to You be the glory. Amen."*

Sidney and Leslie, were sitting behind the defense table. They got up and leaned over the barrier separating them from Jonathon and Annabelle. They hugged Jonathon then exchanging hugs with Annabelle they left the courtroom satisfied with the part they played in Jonathon's defense.

The Bordeaux family sat stunned as they heard the charges against Jonathon. Rose Marie hurried to the defense table and hugged Jonathon. "Praise the Lord," she said turning to Annabelle, "you did a wonderful job, and we are so grateful."

"I had a lot of help," she said gathering her papers and putting them in her briefcase. "Take Jonathon home and celebrate his release. His faith in the Lord has brought the truth out, and he deserves credit for his involvement in his defense, and I think he wants to talk to all of you."

Sandy left as soon as the court was dismissed. She was going to talk to Annabelle about representing her but would save it for another day. She had discovered Robert had hidden money from her and she was sure with the right lawyer she could get her hands on it.

A.J. sat shaking her head in disbelief. She turned to Katrina Louise and said, "Where is the money? Doesn't he have to give it back?"

"A.J., aren't you glad Jonathon doesn't have to go to prison?"

"I guess so, but why don't they give us the money?"

Katrina Louise looked over at Jeffrey, who was shaking his head in disbelief at his little sister's total disconnect with what had just happened.

He wanted to jump up and take Annabelle in his arms. However he knew it would not be advisable under the circumstances. Instead, he sauntered over to the defense table and congratulated his brother then thanked Annabelle for a great job as she smiled, taking his offered hand and giving it a tight squeeze.

ANOTHER BEGINNING

EPILOGUE:

A few days passed before Jeffrey, giving her time, finally called Annabelle. The trial over, Jeffrey told Annabelle he wanted to have a serious talk with her about their future.

"Let's celebrate the end of the trail. How about dinner tonight, you pick the place," he said.

"It's a beautiful day, how about you come over, and we can walk around Jackson Square until we find a place to eat?" Annabelle said, thinking they could talk as they walked. She wanted to have a future with Jeffrey, but she felt like she was cheating on Dean because she still loved him.

They walked hand in hand, stopping to sit on a bench now and then as their conversation presented deeper thought. Jeffrey understood her hesitation to move on and asked if he could do anything to help.

"I think I need to tell Dean about us," Annabelle said.

"What do you mean?" Jeffrey said confused.

"I need to go to Dean's burial place in the Metairie Cemetery."

The trauma of Dean's death stayed with her to this day. They had a wonderful, happy marriage. They complemented each other in every way. They shared their hopes and dreams, then in a flash, he was gone leaving her with a broken heart and destroyed dreams. Now to love another, confused her. Leaving the past behind and moving on to perhaps another great love in her life was almost frightening.

"If you need to go to Dean's gravesite, I will take you there. How about tomorrow morning I pick you up, and we will go to the Cemetery together. But for now, let's enjoy each other's company like you say, it is a beautiful day and we are together," Jeffrey said taking her hand and pulling her up from the bench.

"Good idea, I need to enjoy today and stop living in the past. Thank you, Jeffrey, for your patience with me. I do love you, as surprising as that is for me. I never thought I could love anyone else and now here you are, and I am grateful to God for putting you in my life. So, let's go find a place to have dinner before the sun sets," Annabelle said.

The next morning, Annabelle strolled down the pathway and waited at the gate. Jeffrey got out of the taxi and held the door open letting her in, then went around and got in sitting beside her. Jeffrey took her hand as he told the driver their destination. The drive was in silence as they were both in their own thoughts. Soon the taxi turned and drove through the entrance of the cemetery, then to the mausoleum. Jeffrey got out and opened the door for Annabelle. He gave her a hug and told her he would wait in the taxi.

Annabelle entered the mausoleum, and as she walked toward the niche that held Dean's ashes, her heart began to swell with uncontrollable emotions. The sound of her clicking heels on the marble floor stopped, and she looked at the cold stone covering his burial place, then with a choking sound she let out a breathless cry, "Oh Dean, Leslie is right you'll never be replaced, I loved you more than I could ever tell you. Now I have a chance to love someone else, and it scares me so much."

Suddenly as if an answer to prayer she felt Jeffrey by her side and she asked for God's presence to stay with them as she prayed. *Give me peace Lord that I may overcome this feeling of betrayal. Let me embrace this new person in my life with the joy that only you can bring as my trust in you grows stronger every day. Holy Spirit put in me the wisdom to understand the gift of a new love you have blessed me with and to give you the glory for this relationship. In my Savior Jesus's name, I pray. Amen.*

She placed her hand on the name of her first love engraved in the stone and thanked Jesus for releasing her and giving her peace then turning to Jeffrey she took his hand and smiled letting him know she was ready to spend the rest of her life with him.